I0538527

Educating Anthony

KARA KEEN

EDUCATING ANTHONY
Copyright © 2016 by Kara Keen, LLC

An application to register this book for cataloging has been registered
with the Library of Congress.

All rights reserved. Thank you for supporting writers by buying an
authorized edition of this book and for complying with copyright laws
by not reproducing, scanning or distributing any part of it, with the
exception of reviews of *Educating Anthony* quoting less than 50 words.
For inquiries about the book or Kara Keen, contact us through
www.KaraKeen.com or Kara's Facebook page.

ISBN: 978-0-9743093-9-2

This is a work of fiction. Names, characters, places and incidents either
are the product of the author's imagination or are used fictitiously, and
any resemblance to actual persons, living or dead, business
establishments, events, or locales is entirely complimentary or
coincidental.

Chapter One

Liz

A NTHONY ANZIONE STOOD when I walked into his law office. He's old school that way.

When he came around the desk and shook my hand, I was reminded of his imposing height, the width of his shoulders, and the carefully groomed beard he wore since well before everyone else was doing it. His big, dark eyes, shining with intelligence and humor, drew me in as he put both his hands around mine. It was a very warm, familiar handshake that lingered longer than usual, but not as long as I'd like it to.

"You look well," I said as we sat down. "The past four years since…the funeral, it can't have been easy, and I'm glad to see you're thriving." His impeccable suit and precise haircut, always sexy and longish on top, were exactly as I remembered them. And I didn't even have to look at his feet to know his shoes would be fashionable and shiny. He's an orderly kind of guy.

"Thank you for being there. It meant a lot to me, to all of us." He spoke as if his wife's funeral happened yesterday. It had remained especially vivid and immediate for me as well.

As he always did back when we worked together, he got right to the point. "I see you've developed a great company, Liz, and you did a terrific job for us. I didn't realize it was your public relations firm until you made this appointment."

After an approving glance, he added, "Whatever you're up to, it agrees with you. How can I help you?" His hands were folded on the immaculate desk, his crisp white shirt in sharp contrast to his whiskey brown eyes and dark hair.

It was typical of Anthony's take-charge nature to maneuver the other person into stating their intentions first. Alpha guys like Anthony prefer to let others talk and then deliver their thoughts, strategically fired at the center of the conversation like a missile. I'd seen him do it many times at meetings.

"I need legal help, but not with my PR firm. I own La Vida, a lifestyle nightclub here in Vegas, and I'm exploring the idea of opening other locations. Do you handle that type of business development?"

He sat up straighter, eyebrows raised, his look penetrating. "You own La Vida?"

"I do. The former owners were PR clients." I stifled the urge to cheer at his obvious interest.

"I've handled that type of expansion before, yes. Were you thinking of acquiring competitors, or franchising…what?"

"After you've learned more about La Vida, I'd like to consult with you about those very things."

He tilted back in his chair, his hands clasped behind his head, his face unreadable. "Of course I've heard of La Vida— everyone has—but I'm curious. Is La Vida a swinger's club, a BDSM club, or both?"

"It's both of those things and so much more! I'd love you to be my guest on Saturday night so you can check it out. You'd fit right in."

"And what makes you say that?"

The man excels at playing it cool, but two can play that game.

I leaned forward and shot him a playful grin. "Well, Anthony, I was introduced to the lifestyle years ago by an old boyfriend, back when I was still at Lucid. There was kind of a beginner's night at Mama Lucia's, the lifestyle club back then. Newbies were invited to check out the club, and you and Serena were there." *Gotcha!*

His eyes widened, but he seemed to relax and smile at the pleasant memory. "Yes, she and I learned a lot that night, but we went on to do our own thing at home." He paused, lost in thought, and then looked directly into my eyes. "You were the woman in the gold mask, the one restrained on the wooden rack, weren't you?"

"Yes, that was me," I laughed. "Good memory! How did you know it was me?"

"I remember wondering...I actually just put it together when you mentioned the beginner's night. Your legs—I noticed your legs in those fishnet stockings."

So at some point waaay back then, probably at work, Anthony Anzione had noticed my legs. In detail. And filed the image away in his strategic brain. And remembered it. *Hmmm.*

He must have been reading my mind. "Hey, I was married, not dead, Liz." Adept at avoiding uncomfortable disclosure, he asked "You're a submissive, then?"

"Yes, I enjoy that role, but I'm not hardcore. It's more that I like to play around." I looked in his eyes, waiting for his reaction. All I saw was a slightly raised eyebrow. Anthony had a premium poker face, I had to concede. "Sometimes it's fun to assume the dominant role, and sometimes I'm not in the mood for any kink at all, and I think my open attitude is reflected at La Vida as well.

"We offer a discount to couples who've been together five years or more, the 'Keeping it Fresh' discount. The message is that simply having a fun evening with your spouse is as acceptable at our club as an evening of testing limits and investigating new kinds of kink."

His slight nod told me he was still with me.

"But, Anthony, you recognized the value in a sexy club that night, didn't you? You both had a good time and felt, uh, revitalized…right?"

Of course, in true lawyerly fashion, he nodded without elaborating, and went right back to the action plan. "Then how would this work? I need to know more about your business model."

"The only way to know is to experience it." I'd researched Anthony pretty thoroughly, so I was reasonably sure he wasn't seeing anyone, but my heart still fluttered when I asked him the next question. "Is there anyone you'd like to bring to La Vida?"

"You said I'd be *your* guest Saturday night, right? Let's do that."

His eyes traveled up from his calendar to my lips, triggering a jolt of desire that smoothed out into a slow simmer there.

"That's on the south side, right?" he asked. "Where should I pick you up, and what time?"

We both smiled, aware his response was typically dominant, automatically assuming control. It was also notable that he knew where La Vida was, had probably looked it up on the internet at some point. This was going to be fun!

We stood, and he reached across the pristine glass desk to shake my hand, holding it just a beat too long.

"See you on Saturday night at nine," I said. "I've written my home address on the back of this card."

" Looks like you assumed I'd say yes," he grinned, looking almost like his old self.

I watched his face long enough to see his nostrils flare when I replied, "Actually I keep a few cards like that for when I meet someone special." Striding out in my sexiest spike heels, I was sure he noticed the seams and the Cuban heels on the backs of my stockings.

Anthony was always a fan of friendly competition in the corporate setting, and I could see I got a rise out of him by revealing he might have some competition. It's always good to carry that forward, isn't it?

Chapter Two

Liz

HAVE YOU EVER had a crush on a married guy at work? Experts say (and by experts, I mean your girlfriends) that it's okay as long as—one, you don't act on it, and two, you tell your husband/boyfriend about your crush. The second rule is probably instrumental in helping you observe Rule #One.

Driving home from my meeting with Anthony, I recalled getting ready for a meeting with him six or seven years ago.

My boyfriend Ethan and I were both working for a giant telecommunications company, me in the public relations department, and Ethan in finance. He was looking all sexy and bed-head after a night of ridiculously hot sex, propped up in my bed with a smirk on his face while he watched me dress for work. "Hey Liz," he said, muscular arms flexing as he lounged against the headboard, "ask me how I know you have a meeting with Anthony Anzione today."

Busted! I blushed, embarrassed that Ethan caught me. I mean, it couldn't have been hard to figure out. I had on my favorite blue dress (office appropriate, but form-fitting), high heels, the false eyelashes, and the big hair, all the things I did when I was trying to get someone's attention. (It was years ago, people, so don't judge me about the big hair).

I knew Anthony, head of the legal department, was married, but it was fun to flirt with him anyway. "So…yeah, okay, Ethan. Busted. Joking around with Anthony makes me feel, you know…like I still got a little somethin' somethin'. Does it bother you?" I flounced over to the bed and lay next to Ethan, running my nails over his nipples and batting my eyelashes, all the while trying not to muss my hairdo. Ethan and I hadn't talked about our future as a couple at that point, but I was sure we were a "thing," that our commitment was growing.

His laugh was loud and spontaneous, like everything else about Ethan James. "So you've got a little chemistry experiment going on there. Okay, I don't mind at all…as long as I'm allowed to do the same with the Jessica Alba look-alike in Anzione's office!"

I smacked his chest. "That's not the same at all. She's single." Though I was trying to joke about it, a surge of jealousy made me realize I might be arguing the wrong side of this discussion. Having a married flirt buddy was NOT okay, and in my heart I knew it. Of course, Ethan flirted with pretty much *every* woman, but—duh, me—I excused it by telling myself he had a "flirty personality."

Ethan rewarded my insane logic with another laughing fit. "Oooooh, uh-huh, I see," he quipped, tapping my forehead. "In your mind, it's only okay to tease the married guys. They're supposed to figure out you're not *really* interested, you're just messing with them. Have I got that right?"

I sighed and lay back on the pillow, probably ruining the back of my 'do. "Okay, you're right, but it's just for fun. We chat about legal stuff for work, we joke, he talks about his kids, we talk about life. It's harmless. It's fun. You know he worships his beautiful wife." It was common knowledge the Anziones were devoted to each other, the adorable couple people loved to point out when they were holding hands at the company picnic. "But it's like you mooning over Kate Bosworth in *Blue Crush*. You think I don't notice how many times you've watched that movie? But it's okay, neither of these infatuations are going anywhere."

Of course, Ethan had to say something obnoxious to make me feel insecure, like always. "How do you know that? I might be seeing her on the side." He winked and wiggled his adorable butt at me as he headed into the bathroom, obviously no more threatened by my one-sided crush on Anthony than I was by his obsession with certain sexy, unattainable actresses.

If I'd only known then how prophetic Ethan's comment was, the cheating bastard!

Chapter Three

Liz

"WAS IT GOOD for you, too?"

My doctor was kidding around again, squeezing my hand to reassure me everything would be all right. "All right, time to lie there for a while, let the magic happen." She'd just used something resembling a high-tech turkey baster to insert the previously frozen sperm I ordered from Denmark high up in my uterus, very close to where those eggs of mine were hopefully waiting. It turns out that buying sperm on the internet was as easy as buying shoes! There was about a ten percent chance my eggs would join in "holy baby-making" with the aforementioned sperm, and make me pregnant. If not, there was always next month.

I know, it's insane.

Yesterday I was flirting with a guy I've had a crush on for ten years, hoping he would help me with my business expansion plans—and, let's be honest, my erotic bucket list as well.

Today I'm lying on a table in a doctor's office, praying to become pregnant from donor sperm before I turn forty-one. I've given up looking for Mr. Right in favor of an anonymous donor from Denmark who had been screened for sexually transmitted diseases and genetic disorders. The three principals in this faux conception relationship—me, my friend Lilly, and my doctor—call my donor Lars. Lars's profile says he's in graduate school for his PhD in physics, and is tall, has light brown hair and blue eyes, and his sperm has already helped three women conceive. At first I was startled to learn sperm donors have profiles, just like guys on a dating site, but after the first hour you get used to it, and start entering their files on a spreadsheet.

"How does it look in there, Doc?" I asked. "Is Lars going to need a compass and a power tool to find his way through there?"

"Ohmigod, no," she said. "I checked on them using a microscope, and he has lots of sperm practically jumping off the slide. They've got nice, pointy heads, and wiggly little tails to get through to those eggs of yours. You're ovulating nicely, and you've been taking your Clomid, right?"

"Right." My tubes had been checked, and all other systems were go. The doc made it sound like sperm-seeking-egg was a colorful new video game to play on my smartphone.

Checking the laptop with all my info, the doc said "Why did you go with Lars, if you don't mind my asking?"

"Primarily because I didn't want to use some random dude who could have diseases and later pop up and make my life miserable by claiming parental rights!"

She threw up her hands. "From your mouth to God's ears! If only all women who want to get pregnant were as smart! Some of the women I work with spend more time buying a handbag than figuring out who should father their child."

Now Lilly joined in. "I have a friend who used a friend, and now that guy and his idiot girlfriend are testing their child-raising theories on her adorable daughter two weekends a month! And that's after my friend spent a fortune on legal fees!"

I shuddered at the very thought, thankful I had the money for this carefully planned procedure. "Number two consideration is that I don't want to run into the guy, even in an airport, if at all possible. I can't imagine ever attending a physics conference, and I want being a mommy to be on my terms. Number three and four are—wait for it—the Danes do a great job with the screening, collecting, and freezing thing, and, last but not least, my mom's maiden name is Jensen, and her people are from Denmark."

We all nodded and I went back to staring up at the ceiling tiles, willing my body to relax. Shifting a little, crinkling the paper as I twisted my pelvis up, I hoped to encourage those little spermies to swim upstream and make themselves at home in one of my friendly, comfortable eggs.

I knew I'd arrived late to the baby-making party, thinking these last few years I'd meet the true love who'd want what I only recently discovered I wanted—the full family partnership, the whole nine yards. Soccer practice, the minivan, a few precious weekends away for Mom and Dad. Huh! Who'da thought?

When you're the oldest of six, you grow up being a mommy. You're always running around making things okay for everyone else, as all mommies do. When I left home at 18, I declared I was done with raising kids for life. I was offended every time someone told me I'd change my mind, and I still don't understand why a discussion about what I do with my lady parts can be considered a legit topic of casual conversation. Then a few years ago my clock started ticking…loudly.

My friend Lilly had it even worse than I did. She was the oldest of thirteen kids living in a farm cult in Texas. She had to help with the younger ones, AND milk the cow, AND chop the wood…you get the picture. If you could see her now, from her expensive hair extensions to her Jimmy Choo heels, you'd say "This chick has never seen the business end of a diaper or a cow," but you'd be wrong.

Lilly was totally with me, both physically and mentally. We've shared wild and crazy times but, truth be told, she does me ten times better in the wild department. She's the only woman I know who's gone to a wedding in New Orleans and slept with all three men in the wedding party, including the groom. In her defense, she didn't know he was the groom at the time.

More than anyone, Lilly knew exactly where I was coming from, and probably wondered why the hell I was lying here waiting for a random Viking sperm to swim vigorously upstream to my egg.

"How about some sperm jokes?" she asked me. "I memorized them especially for this occasion!" She cracked herself up, launching into them before I answered. "Why does it take millions of sperm to fertilize one egg? Because sperm won't ask for directions, either! Wait, here's a better one. How can you tell if a man has a high sperm count? You have to chew before you swallow!"

The doctor was laughing, too, even though she told us later she'd heard them all before. "You said you had twins in your family. What was it like when the twins were little?" she asked, encouraging me to talk, because she knew I was anxious. "Just lie still while you tell us about mothering twins. It could be happening right now!"

Memories piled on about caring for my twin brothers, Cole and Jack, when I was barely three and they were newborns. "I used to make marks on a little chart in their room…when they had a bottle, when they had a diaper change. Can you imagine a three-year-old doing that? I ran around bringing my mom diapers and bottles, but probably my biggest contribution was being *such* a good girl and growing up really, really fast! I was toilet trained at a year and a half, and reading *Go Dog Go* to Cole and Jack at three."

I had never even imagined having twins, but when I thought about my twin siblings Cole and Jack, and the other set, Anne and Ariana, I was…psyched! Remembering their secret twin languages, and how my mom used to put nail polish on Cole's toe so we could tell them apart, never failed to make me laugh.

"Carrying twins would probably suck," I said to Lilly, "and caring for them the first year would be like managing a moon launch, but hell, my twin brothers and sisters are some of the most amazing people I know. Who wouldn't wanna make *that* happen?!" I wondered if my mom would team up with me the way I helped her, but our bond could withstand whatever she decided at this point. My close relationship with her was its own reward.

"Girl, you are *in* this thing if you're ready to do *that*!" Lilly laughed and walked around to the head of the table, giving my shoulders a little massage. "Blow out a big breath, relax, and imagine little Lars being born, soft music playing in a darkened room. They'll want you to be calm, because he'll probably be three feet long at birth. They'll be pulling him out of you hand over hand."

People say you don't know what you've got until it's gone, and while I lay there, sharing family stories with Lilly, I realized it was true. Kissing boo-boos, nuking chicken nuggets, and promoting the merits of pooping on the toilet seemed like a pain in the ass when I was actually doing it, but recently I realized they were part of the weirdest, most awesome head game ever invented—being a parent. Little kids need your attention sixty times a day, and I've decided that is the reward, not the punishment!

I've struggled for so long to be free, free of my family's need for an extra set of hands, free of the constraints of working for someone else, free to explore my sexual options and develop my businesses at the same time. I spent years focused on myself and the things I thought would make me happy, and I believed I'd built a great life for myself, a life as different from my parents as I could make it…but it ended up not being enough.

Recently I've felt like a leaf in the wind, too free for anyone to care about. A script from growing up is running in the back of my head, the one where you earn the right to care for someone. I wanted to be needed, to be a crucial part of someone's life. I wanted a little person to cuddle with who would mess up my carefully laid plans. I wanted that little person to look at me with trust and love, to depend on me for all her physical and emotional needs.

Had I become like my mother, the neurons in my brain following the age-old path to female happiness? Will I hear her words come out of my mouth, those familiar phrases from childhood I swore I would never use? It's funny, but at that point I didn't care! I knew I wanted it, and I couldn't see anything else.

Except maybe Anthony. I could see him as…I didn't know what. "How did your meeting with the attorney go?" Lilly asked.

"It went great. He's coming to La Vida with me on Saturday night to, uh, check out the business model."

Lilly stared at me for beat. "Wait a minute. Is this *that* attorney, the guy you had a crush on a million years ago?! I thought you had sworn off dating, woman! How does this fit with the reason you're lying on this table?" Obviously

Lilly knew me—and my history—way too well.

I wondered if I should be embarrassed by the way I'd gone after Anthony, boldly canvassing his office for the initial business, and then waltzing in there with the La Vida proposition.

It was seduction, pure and simple...at a time when seduction made zero sense! What saved me was that I truly did want his opinion, and I accepted it would be brutally honest. I like brutally honest. Especially if it keeps me from doing something stupid that costs me time, money, and heartache.

"It doesn't fit at all," I said, "except I trust him to be straight with me about the expansion plans for La Vida. The rest...a sexy guy I used to have a crush on is now available, and he seems interested. Men do this stuff all the time, so there must be something to it! Call it a fling, call it unfinished business. Whatever."

Lilly shook her head, squinting at me. "I just don't want to call it another broken heart, okay?"

I sighed. It sounded like a big-ass sigh, even to me. "I didn't realize it myself until recently, but I've been waiting to do this with him, to find out if there's anything there. Ever since his wife died, I've wondered..."

Chapter Four

Anthony

LIZ'S BUILDING WASN'T what I expected, and, believe me, I spent way too much time thinking about her after she visited my office. Picture a steel and glass high-rise, elegant and intimidating, hulking doorman in the lobby—that's what I envisioned. Kind of the condo equivalent of her expensive high heels and pencil skirts. This wasn't anything like what I'd imagined.

I parked in a spot marked "visitor," next to a neat row of numbered parking spaces filled with minivans, old sedans, and pickup trucks with ladders attached. The space I walked into was a leafy courtyard in the center of a large, two-story, hacienda-style building with arched balconies. Purple bougainvillea hung over the railings, and the stucco was painted a spicy clay color, with dark columns, and a terra-cotta tile roof. Around a central fountain, kids pulled each other in a red wagon, laughing and screaming "Es mi turno! Es mi turno!" while an elderly Indian woman with a bindi read the newspaper in a shady corner.

Leaning over the upper balcony and talking to the kids in Spanish was Liz, who pointed at a stairway to my right when she saw me. "I'm up here, Anthony, and the stairs are over there," she called to me, and when I got to the top she was waiting for me. "Come in, let's talk before we go." Her voice trailed off as she walked through a door behind her, leaving it open for me. Except for a bright Mexican rug and an enormous, carved fireplace, everything was modern in her home. She turned and saw me taking it all in. Spreading her arms, she asked "So? What do you think of mí casa?"

Her hair was up in a twist again, and she was wearing red heels, a red dress, and dark, seamed stockings I suspected were held up by a garter belt. Her cheeks were flushed, and she had on a pair of reading glasses, generating a hot librarian vibe.

"That dress, everything about you…" I let out a low whistle. She smiled, actually blushing a little. "And your place is…not what I expected. I was thinking high-rise for some reason." I hoped she would take it the right way.

She did. Nodding, she went behind her kitchen island and took out two wine glasses and a bottle. "Red okay?" she asked. "I like your car. A Jaguar 12-cylinder, right?"

"Yeah, I don't get to drive it all-out much, but it's nice to be able to afford it now I'm only paying one college tuition." I grabbed the corkscrew and opened and poured the wine, glad to have something to do with my hands. My fingers itched to touch her. I always thought she was attractive back when we worked together, but it was nuts how much I'd thought about her over the past few days. She looked so beautiful tonight, sexy as hell.

Chuckling, she took a sip and said, "I actually bought this building, hoping to move the club here. When the neighborhood behind us got wind of it, they freaked out and influenced the zoning board to turn down my application for a parking variance, blocking the whole plan."

When she drank more wine and licked her lips, it was a struggle to focus on what she was saying, but now she was full-on laughing. "An apartment building down the street burned down, and I was able to rush through an affordable housing application to move five families in here." This cracked her up so much, she put her wine down, her hand on the counter for support. Her husky laugh was another thing I'd forgotten about. It was the kind that made you want to join in.

Her laugh also had a way of pulling me out of rational thought, but suddenly it occurred to me why this was so funny. "I'll bet that pissed off your uppity neighbors, didn't it?"

"Oh, my God, yes, you *get* it! It's their worst nightmare." Still quaking with laughter, she smoothed her dress, calming herself. I'd forgotten about her enormous smile and the way she chattered on when she was nervous. "Don't you hate snobs?! But you know, I'm the one who totally lucked out. These neighbors of mine are *the best*. The guy downstairs from me, Vlad, he's the superintendent, and he can fix anything. Everybody pays on time, they're super neat, and so nice."

"I think they're very grateful to be living in such a nice place with such a considerate landlord," I said.

I'd also forgotten her reputation for kindness. She'd organized a charity event at work back in the day, and received an award for attracting recent veterans to our internship program. Now here she was, providing a great space to live for a group of people who had needed it desperately. I wasn't sure exactly why, but the way she turned her interests into successful businesses turned me on. Maybe because she had so much fun doing it?

"Shhhh." She held a finger to her lips. "They don't know I own the building, so mum's the word, okay?"

EDUCATING ANTHONY | 19

"Got it." I couldn't help myself, I needed to see where I stood sooner, not later. I put my hand over hers. "Liz, I…I hope you don't just think of me as your attorney. I'd like to be more." This was someone very different from the girl who used to talk too much in my office, and I supposed we'd both changed.

Her eyes went soft and the giggle disappeared. "You already *are* more, Anthony. You've always been more." Okay, she surprised me with that one, but not so much that I didn't reach for her arm and draw her close to me. She put her hands on my chest, her palms warming me through my dress shirt until I felt my skin was on fire. "Do you think I'm strange, being so direct?"

"I think we're both grown-ups, and we can be as direct as we want to be." When I cradled the back of her neck in my hand, she turned her face up to mine.

"I hope I can kiss you," I said, "because you smell as amazing as you look." When our lips met, hers were welcoming and somehow familiar, tasting of wine and temptation. Kissing her felt like the most natural thing in the world, like a wake-up call to the dead man walking I'd been for the past four years. She kissed me back, and the rush of heat straight to my groin caught me by surprise.

Touching her felt wonderful, and I curved my arm around her waist, my hand resting on the curve of her ass. She pressed against me and exhaled a long breath.

"I've been wanting to do that since the day I met you," she sighed.

I liked that she was tall enough that we fit together beautifully. "Kiss me?" I asked, not leaving an inch between us, not wanting her to pull away. My lips were on her neck now, exploring exactly where that fragrance of hers was coming from.

"We were in a hotel gym, at Lucid's annual convention." She leaned back, breaking me out of my trance and grinning up into my face. "I watched you while you were lifting weights and practically turned cartwheels to get you to notice me. You never did."

"I noticed you. You were wearing a T-shirt from the company marathon. And you used to always have a spray tan. I did, too. I remember we were all kind of orange in those days."

She nodded, a smile quirking the corner of her mouth. "Yes, it was 2008. You couldn't be too orange in 2008!"

"Anyway, of course I noticed you, Liz, but…"

"I know. You weren't wearing your wedding ring in the gym, so I checked around and found out the bad news. It's okay, I get it." She'd moved away and was sipping her wine again, obviously feeling guilty. *We weren't ready to address the elephant in the room yet, and why should we? We noticed each other when I was married to Serena. Was that a crime, or just a common factor in people's lives? Do we honestly believe our attraction to other people vanishes the minute we walk down the aisle?*

"But you still made appointments, came in and talked about some of the events with me." I tried to not sound accusing, but I was very curious about her intent back then.

"You made me…feel things. I couldn't help myself. I hoped we would transition to kind of a brotherly thing, and you really did give me great advice! I could've emailed you, of course, but…well, you know."

"Yes, unfortunately, I do know. Like I said in my office, I was married, not dead. It was torture at times, but…I think a lot of married people struggle with attraction."

"Ethan, my boyfriend at the time, called me on it once. He saw me getting all dolled up for work and told me he knew I would be seeing you that day."

EDUCATING ANTHONY | 21

"Ethan James? He was your boyfriend?" I couldn't help myself, I had to comment. "Sorry, but that guy is a dick! Did you know he was siphoning off money from a company scholarship fund into a private account?"

"No! Really? Huh." She looked thoughtful while she gathered up her purse and a laptop case. "Well...I'm not surprised. He was secretly engaged to a woman in Los Angeles the entire time we were together. Gave me the 'I'm working out of the LA office' line when he disappeared. Asshole."

I admired her bravado about Ethan's terrible betrayal, but I sensed it had affected her more than she let on. It seemed like she was hiding something else, too, something big, but I was still too hot from her kiss to ask questions. "The embezzlement thing happened shortly after you left, and I had the pleasure of escorting Ethan from the building myself. For some reason, the company only fired him and didn't press charges, maybe because he returned all the money." I dangled my keys. "I'll drive, since you've been enjoying your vino."

"Thanks, I was counting on it." I carried her laptop, and she waved to some of her neighbors as we walked out to the parking lot. When I opened the car door and she got in, she winked up at me and said, "By the way, I never did transition to that brotherly feeling. You don't feel like my brother at all. I guess I was playing a long, long game and didn't even know it. That's okay, isn't it?"

I was holding her hand while she sank into the low-slung seat of my car. I raised her fingers to my lips and kissed them. "Perfectly okay. I have a sister, and you don't feel like a sister at all, Liz."

On the way there, I added, "I don't know why I didn't call you sooner, but I'm glad you got back in touch. Maybe now, with my girls off and doing their thing, is the best time for us to meet again." Chuckling, I added, "Now I've shed the cook, chauffeur, and nurse duties of parenting, I have to admit I've needed some…somebody to hang out with." God, that comment was lame, but it's been a while since I had to talk about *feelings*.

La Vida was in a warehouse/office district that looked like any other, busy with tradesmen and deliveries on weekdays, and deserted at night and on weekends. Perfect for a business like La Vida that needed plenty of parking and operated Thursday through Monday after 9 pm. We'd talked numbers on the way over, and Liz was making good money here, with a low mortgage, and commercial neighbors who didn't bother her. "Why are you open Sundays and Mondays?" I asked.

"It's a Vegas thing. Tourists and convention attendees extend their weekends into Mondays, so Tuesday and Wednesday are the slow days. Even the big shows are open on Sunday and Monday nights."

I'd been doing a little homework. "I looked at lifestyle clubs in other cities, and most of them, if not all, are only open Thursday through Saturday. You have two more nights of profitability here in Vegas you wouldn't have elsewhere. In other cities, the Thursdays are usually 35-and-under nights, with varying degrees of success. And the referrals you get from some of the Vegas hotels, restaurants, convention centers and limo drivers are a big deal. And there is the fact that this is Sin City, so people come here to be…you know, to have fun." I put my hand on her shoulder to reassure her, since I knew none of it was good news for her expansion plans. "You have to admit, it wouldn't be the same in, say, Orlando."

She sighed as we pulled up to the club. "I know all this, but when you lay it out…"

A vaguely military-looking guy with a brush cut—a bouncer, I assumed—was waiting for her, holding open the front door. His eyes burned through me, and I felt a twinge of jealousy, wondering if he and Liz were ever together. *Was this how it was going to be? I would be constantly wary of every man in her life?* Such feelings were very new to me, because Serena and I were each other's first and only, and no one since then had mattered. Until now.

"There's another thing that has to do with being in Vegas, actually, which you'll want to check out later," Liz said, looking thoughtful.

I took her hand to help her up the stairs in those high heels. "I'm sorry to deliver so many negative observations tonight. I haven't even walked in the door of La Vida yet."

I'd gotten great news, though. She had feelings for me. Every time I looked in her eyes, I saw desire, need and…yes. It was what I'd hoped for since she walked into my office four days ago. Before that as well. In fact, every time I remembered her over the past few years.

Liz rushed ahead of me and embraced a woman she knew. "Lilly! I'm so glad you're here tonight! This is Anthony Anzione, the attorney I told you about." Her friend, a platinum blonde with pale skin who was all red lips and big, brown eyes, was unabashedly checking me out, clearly another Liz-fan who seemed very protective of her.

"You guys are paisanos," Liz added. "Anthony, meet Lilly Ciccone, my best friend since middle school. And, yes, she is related to *that* Madonna, Madonna Ciccone." I had to admit, she did resemble Madonna from back in the *You Can Dance* days.

I felt better when Lilly gave me a friendly hug. "Hey,

Anthony, nice to meet you. Yes, Madonna is a third cousin twice removed, and yes, I've heard only good things about you."

"Guys, excuse me, I have to take this call up in my office." Liz backed away with her phone against her ear. "Lilly, would you walk him over to the ballroom, explain the alcohol thing?"

"I actually read about the couples-only and the bring-your-own-booze thing on the website," I said as Lilly and I walked past other couples checking in near a classy brass fountain in the lobby. "It makes the membership dues very important, since La Vida can't make money on booze or gambling. My dad belonged to the local Italian-American social club, and it had the same setup." I knew a liquor license wasn't necessary for this kind of club, because the club only provides orange juice, soda, and other setups for the alcohol.

"Yeah, my dad did, too!" Lilly laughed. "It works well, and means it's a much less regulated nightclub this way. They have my bottle of Jack behind the bar, so does a Jack and Coke work for you?" I nodded. The bartender knew her, and we walked into the ballroom, drinks in hand.

Like many clubs, La Vida's ballroom was in a large warehouse space dominated by flashing lights and the powerful beat of dance music. There was a seductive fragrance in the air, and the room was surrounded by floor-to-ceiling screens showing sexy music videos, one of which represented the title currently playing. The end result was that the entire crowd seemed to be dancing, laughing, and having fun, most dressed in skimpy club wear. It was like any other nightclub, but without the predatory males stalking around, since only couples were admitted. Some people—both women and men—were topless, and there was a lot of touching and embracing going on. A stripper pole and a cage on one end of the room showcased some amazing, professional-looking dancers who also circulated through the crowd, whipping any reluctant dancers into a frenzy.

Lilly drifted away to dance with friends, and Liz showed up with another drink for me and a pink martini, clutching it a little too tightly, her voice shaky. Leaning in to speak in my ear over the music, she said "That's the other Vegas factor I have going on here, those gorgeous dancers. They're from a dance show at the Boca Casino called *Romancing Vegas*, and my brother's future sister-in-law is the producer. People love to look at them, so they all get in for free and, lucky for me, they treat La Vida like their private playground."

"What was the call about? Everything okay?" I asked her. She was glossing over something, but seemed upset.

"Oh…uh, dammit!" She tilted her head back and drained her drink. "I have neighbors here in this office park who are harassing me. Two lawyers." Slamming her glass down on the table, she said, "Their space here is an antique business, and they're circulating a petition to get rid of me, to get rid of La Vida."

"That *is* harassment." I said. "What's the problem?"

Liz shrugged and blew out a big breath. "It started when someone spray-painted their truck and then…" One of the dancers came over and put his arms around both us, swinging us out on the floor, determined to put a smile on our faces. "Sorry. Let's forget about it for now," she laughed and snuggled into my neck when the music slowed.

Chapter Five

Liz

THE MOMENT ANTHONY'S hand settled on my butt at the condo, raw desire for him erupted, and continued to pulse through me. Okay, before that too, but still...

As we walked around the club, I heard myself saying "Look at this," and "What do you think about that?" and I felt myself smiling and greeting people, but it was like watching a television show of someone else's life, someone who didn't care so much about this handsome, charismatic man. Every female in the club was eye-fucking him, checking out those long, restless strides of his. I struggled to keep up in my sky-high heels, and recalled how out of place he'd sometimes seemed when he was prowling around the office, stalking whatever he required, as if he needed to be released from captivity immediately.

We danced for a couple of songs, and I probably shouldn't have been surprised by what a good dancer he was. I had only gotten as far as hoping he wouldn't do the side-to-side shuffle (boring in bed?) or the flailing arms and legs (watch me trying hard!).

Instead, he committed to me and to the music, dirty-dancing me from the front and the back, unexpectedly grinding the shit out of it.

He rocked some actual, real dance steps to Rihanna's *Hate How Much I Love You*, whirling me in and out with a big smile. I had the sense I was closely watching him while he was closely watching me, but he seemed unexpectedly lighthearted and up for a good time.

I went to the ladies' room, and, of course checked all the stalls and the sinks for cleanliness and supplies (business owner behavior), but when I came out, Lilly was there. "I saw you dancing," she gasped, "and I'm speechless. I figured, you know, he was older, and he was married for a long time—I figured you'd be waaay out of his league in the hotness department. But he's not the starched white shirt he appears to be! You said he has grown-up daughters; how old did you say he is?!"

"Mother Google says forty-five; he was married in college at nineteen." Lilly knew the whole story with Serena, just not the numbers. I'd become the resident expert, obviously.

When I came back, a young couple was hitting on him, and they brought me into the conversation, apparently hoping to get lucky with the hottest alpha dog in the room. And who could blame them? I tug=ged him away, and he murmured "Saved by the teacher!" in my ear. He was a good kind of slightly drunk guy, happy and less inhibited, but not sloppy.

Holding his upper arm and laying my cheek on his shoulder, I replied, "I'm not sure who's the teacher and who's the student here. You're such an awesome dancer! Are you ready to see the private rooms there, Usher?"

He laughed and let me lead the way, putting his arm around me and squeezing. His easy affection disarmed me. In the past, we'd known each other in a formal office context, filled with booby traps and no-no's. This warm, sexy Anthony was a revelation…and a temptation.

We cruised the alcoves surrounding the ballroom, some with their glittery curtains closed for privacy. Others were open so we could see the mostly-nude couples inside, doing their thing on the padded platforms. Anthony seemed to understand the "watching and being watched" thing perfectly, watching and making eye contact if the person was looking for it, or not, giving the subtle head nod and moving on.

I could feel him holding back questions, knowing it was too soon to ask what and who *I* had done in this club of mine. "I've only owned this place for a year, so in case you're wondering, no, I haven't done most of this stuff. Too busy doing the work," I said ruefully.

The Trey Songz tune *I Invented Sex* was on, and I chuckled, holding up a hand and pledging "I swear, I did not invent sex." His lips were twitching as he struggled to hide a smile at my astute mind reading.

Touring him around the private VIP activity suites, I felt as if I wasn't educating Anthony, but rather, he was somehow educating me. Yes, he had been with one woman most of his life, and I had been in a series of relationships, but it didn't mean he hadn't experienced most of the same things I had. Since I had never been in a long long-term relationship the way he had (three years was my longest), he might understandably be wondering if I even had the skills to sustain a long-term, loving partnership. I wished *I* knew.

It was early in the evening, so most people were still upstairs dancing, and we had most of the rooms to ourselves. In the dungeon, he ran his hands over the wooden rack they call the St. Andrew's Cross, shooting me a knowing look. "Someday I'd like to recreate the night I saw you on this thing." He leaned under the spanking bench, examining the construction, and shook the bars of the fake cage. I liked the way he seemed compelled to touch everything. I was willing to bet he was one of these guys who liked to build things.

"What's this thing?" he asked, tugging on the ropes hanging from a long, sturdy wooden beam on the ceiling.

"It's for *shibari*, Japanese rope bondage. We have a famous photographer coming in Friday who's also a practitioner." I showed him some photos on my phone of men and women tied up with intricate patterns of knots and overlapping ropes, suspended from a frame. Some were naked, some were clothed. "I'm told it's very calming to be bound and suspended like that, and people often float out into the subspaces of the mind. I've volunteered to be one of his subjects."

I could tell he was conflicted, choosing his words carefully. "I'm intrigued. That's...amazingly hot. Will you be naked or...?"

Interrupting him, I said "I was thinking about wearing a black fishnet body stocking, since my skin is kind of sensitive. What do you think?"

"I think I'd like to be here for that," he said, his smile wavering a little.

"Absolutely!" I said. "We'll probably have a good crowd here. So...moving on?"

When I showed him the massage room, there was a group there. They'd left the curtain and the window open, signaling their willingness for others to watch and listen. Anthony stood behind me, kissing my neck and touching me while we watched two naked couples massage a nude woman lying facedown on a massage table. Another man, presumably her partner, seemed to be directing the action, calling her Delia. Delia whimpered softly while everyone's hands touched her body, soothing her with fragrant oil, with one of the men massaging her feet while rubbing them against his penis.

Delia thrust upwards toward two men who were rubbing the lush globes of her bottom. Squeezing them and pulling them apart, the men poured warm oil on her anus and began to massage it, one of them exploring it with his fingers as her sighing grew louder.

When she turned onto her back, the mood seemed to change, and she moaned loudly as the hands touching her body turned greedy, the two women pinching and stroking her breasts, then licking and sucking them. I felt Anthony's mood change, too, his erection hard and thick, pressing into me as he kissed the sensitive skin behind my ear. "I'm extremely good at massage," he growled in my ear.

When one of the men began to lick and suck Delia's pussy and another put his dick near her face, I turned toward Anthony and grabbed his shirt, pulling his mouth roughly against mine. He felt so good, and the second his tongue brushed against mine, I let my body react to his smell, the feel of his beard feathering across my skin and the heavy ache between my legs. Whew! I felt myself fighting the urge to climb him right then and there, to touch him in more places. Instead, I pulled away, both of us fully aware of what was happening here.

"Moving on?" I asked, my voice husky and my lips already feeling swollen from his knowing kisses.

He took my hand so sweetly. "Moving on," he nodded, and we both laughed.

The windows to the orgy room are always open; I mean, if you want to be part of an orgy, you want to be seen, right? A large round bed with red sheets and pillows dominated the center of the room, where a voluptuous blonde with enormous breasts was being pleasured by two men. Music and laughter came from the room, along with sighs, screams, and slaps. A woman on the padded platform to our right enthusiastically sucked on one cock while another man entered her from behind, and other attractive couples and groups were involved in all kinds of kinky fuckery.

Anthony's breathing was rapid behind me, one hand wandering under the neckline of my dress, the other cupping and squeezing my ass. The simmering chemistry and attraction between us was rapidly coming to the boiling point. "Do you imagine yourself doing this? Does it turn you on?"

I felt like the subtext of his question was "*Have* you done this?"

"I like being dirty in front of people with my lover," I said. "I have felt aroused, sometimes felt...liberated...being watched by others. And...you know...I might *think* about a group thing, or men lining up to fuck me. But in real life," I shrugged, "no, not so much. Don't you think this is like watching porn, though, only hotter?"

"I can think of something even hotter right now. But yes, it's very, very hot. Hotter than a nightclub, and more fun than the place in the movie *Eyes Wide Shut*. That seemed way too serious, didn't it?"

The curtains were closed in the next several rooms, but we heard voices inside. "How do you make sure everything happening in these rooms is consensual?" Anthony asked.

"Do you remember the consent form you signed before you came into the club? It clearly states, in bold letters, that the private rooms are monitored with listening devices, and cameras can be activated if the management deems it necessary."

"Right, right, yes," Anthony said. "As a matter of fact, your guy at the desk, the one who went through the paperwork with me, had highlighted that section and pointed it out to me. I think it's a good method, emphasizing the information that way, and the fact that it was one guy explaining the rules to another guy. It's going to make men think twice before they play outside the lines."

"I had no idea he was doing that. What an excellent way to handle it." I tapped the details into my phone, wanting to remember to acknowledge his approach later. "He and his wife both work here part-time, and they first came here as members before I bought the place."

"Correct me if I'm wrong, here, but the place seems very woman-centered, very safe for women, and I think that's your influence. And you seem to have good people on your staff, so important. Have you ever, uh, the men who work here, have you..."

I had to rescue him from his obvious discomfort. "No, Anthony, I haven't been involved in any way with anyone who works here. Feel better now?"

"Yes," he said with a hiss, tugging me back against chest. His move surprised me, and I was a little off balance, turning and putting my arms around his neck. "I don't share," he murmured, raising goose bumps by brushing his beard and breathing across the sensitive spot below my ear. "Does that bother you?"

"Nnn...no," I said, oddly pleased by his preference. I kissed along his jaw and down his neck the way he'd been kissing me.

"Then I think you should show me your office. Right now."

As soon as he kicked the door shut behind us, Anthony grabbed my hips and walked me backward until I was against the wall, his body pressing tight to mine. His arms caged me, his hands against the wall on either side of my head. His lips felt as hot as they looked, crashing down on mine, fierce and intense. He angled his head, deepening the kiss, and pushing me tight to the wall, his hands in my hair, his mouth everywhere. He seemed unable to stop as he kissed along my neck, holding my head just tightly enough that I couldn't kiss him back. For some reason, that turned me on. He stared at me, sweat beading along his brow. "This isn't how I wanted it, but I have to fuck you right now. I'll take better care of you later."

I closed my eyes and savored the feel of him, drunk on the knowledge that he was out of control...for me. Anthony Anzione, Mr. Cool, was acting crazy. Because of me. I assumed he was a control freak...control the setting, control me, control his response. But here we were, in a mutual frenzy, our desire raw and real and up against the wall.

Need spiraled through me, and I anticipated the next touch and the next as he kissed me deep and hard, his lips moving down to work some crazy magic on my nipples right through my dress. He was shaking, his breath coming in ragged pants, as his big hands gripped my waist and he rocked his hips against mine.

Pulling the sash on my dress, his eyes went wide when he saw my breasts, ripe fruit for him to enjoy. "My God, Liz, so beautiful," he breathed, and immediately put his hands on them, cupping them, my nipples tight again at his touch. My arms locked around his neck, and he kissed me again, letting me open his shirt while his whiskers rubbed against my skin.

The tension rose between us, and he gasped when I ran my hand over his erection, which was straining against the fabric of his slacks. "Are you ready to finish what you started here?" he asked.

Loving the low tone in his voice, I murmured "A girl can only hope," breathing against his neck.

"Take your dress off." I made a show of throwing it across

the room, and he hitched me up harder against the wall. I froze, now even more aroused by the rough authority in his voice. No more flirty bullshit, this was *ON!*

Dragging my nails down his chest, I reveled in his husky moan and the way he inhaled when his nipples pebbled like mine. I wanted to find a bed, but this thing was happening right here, right now. I couldn't remember anyone fucking me up against the wall, ever. The truth of it thrilled me.

His flat palms pushing my legs wide in front of him, he roughly slid his hands down, then tucked his fingers under the elastic of my garter belt. *Snap!* "That's been driving me crazy all evening," he groaned. "These too," he said digging his fingers into my hair and taking out all the pins, one by one, kind of dragging it out. I didn't even have to shake it out; he seemed to enjoy running his fingers through it. His focus amped me up and he leaned forward to kiss me senseless while he arranged it on my shoulders.

"Damn, Liz, look at you." Admiring my shaved, naked pussy, Anthony had flicked the switch and gone into full-on Dominant mode. His rough hands slid between my legs, thumbing my clit and pushing fingers into me, first one and then two fingers, exploring and exciting every secret place inside me. "You are so fucking wet," he groaned.

I flinched but pressed closer to him when he teased my nipples with his teeth and his tongue, seeming to understand how hard, how fast, and how wet I wanted his mouth. When his fingers found the cushy spot inside me, I felt my orgasm building. He withdrew his fingers, leaving me aching for him as he stepped out of his boxers and trousers and shrugged his shirt onto the floor.

He watched me as he tore the condom packet open with his teeth, trying to hide a smile when I gasped at the thickness of his dick when he rolled it on. He hauled me up higher on the wall, pressing that beautiful, naked body of his between my legs. "Wrap your legs around me." His fierce command made me tremble. When he thrust deep inside me, I cried out from pure lust, every nerve inside me tuned to his beautiful cock.

The full feeling of him inside me was surprising, his hips slapping against my thighs, bouncing me against the wall. After only a few rough, addictive strokes, I was shocked when I gasped, my muscles seized, and my head fell back while I came. No bed, no fancy foreplay, just the slow surge and relentless rhythm of this utterly frantic attraction.

Pulling me close to him, he breathed me in as he carried me over to my desk and laid me on it, shoving papers off onto the floor.

"You like this, that you can make me fuck you this way, don't you?" he hissed, teeth gritted. I could only groan in response, struggling to form words as he shook my entire body with every thrust. I closed my eyes to focus on the sensation while he thrust deeper and deeper into me.

Leaning closer, he put four fingers flat across my clit, circling with the perfect pressure as my pussy clenched around his cock. "Open your eyes and come, Liz, come for me now!"

When he pinched my ass I came again, jerking around him as he rumbled an *"Aaaaahhmmmm!"* and his strokes grew urgent, short and fast, as he joined me in Blissland. When he finished gasping for air, I sat up and snuggled my head into his belly, running my fingers in the patterns of his six-pack.

He was looking down at me, male satisfaction all over his face, when I locked eyes with him and said "Moving on?"

We were both still laughing when we sneaked out the back door of the club so no one would see me, my wanton hair and messed-up clothes providing more information than anyone needed.

When he pulled up to my place, the song *Take Me to Church* was on. Answering the question in his eyes, I said "Of course, come on in. You said you were going to take better care of me later so let's go…worship in my bedroom." And we did.

Chapter Six

Anthony

NO WAY WAS I going to watch that photographer, Zane Wilson, tie up Liz at his presentation at La Vida. Absolutely not happening. I went to his website and saw he was looking for volunteers, so I volunteered to be his apprentice for the night.

After a quick study of some hot Tumblr blogs, I bought some soft red rope at Home Depot, imagining how it would look against the black fishnet body stocking she planned to wear. The woman who checked me out was checking me out, and I could swear she blushed, looking from me to the rope and back. Seemed like everyone and their grandmother was into this since *Fifty Shades of Grey*.

I was a scout when I was a kid, but the knots they tied on these blogs went way beyond that. I finally compromised with a wrapping and tying plan I submitted to the photographer, and after making a few changes, he approved it.

La Vida ended up hosting a spontaneous masked ball-type event that night, and most of the people were wearing masks or intricate face makeup. Normally, there was absolutely no photography permitted at the club, but since Zane Wilson planned to photograph his demonstration, people were covering or disguising their faces.

Yes, we were all there to do our own version of the wild thing, but certainly no one wanted to be photographed doing it, including me. I found a black silk half mask that was surprisingly comfortable and wore a suit I could move around in easily while I tied my ropes.

Zane Wilson turned out to be a genuinely nice guy, and he was okay with the idea that I would be the only one to touch Liz. "So is this a new thing, you and Liz?" he asked.

"Yeah, very new," I said, wondering if this guy had ever been with her. When he introduced me to the guy he'd be tying up tonight as his husband, my gut stopped churning around that question at least.

He showed me a trio of sturdy ropes he'd suspended from parallel beams on the ceiling, looking at me and adjusting their height. "I'm glad you want to do this, Anthony. But since you're too inexperienced to safely do a suspension from scratch, I made this rope cradle for you to lie her in. Just signal me when you're ready toward the end of the demo." He pointed up to the ceiling. "I wanted to show people this simple way to use the same hardware you'd use for a porch swing."

A suspension? Wow, I was feeling cooler by the second! I hung out in the darkened hallway, waiting for Liz while people gathered around the photographer and his ropes.

"Shibari is the Japanese art of decorative rope binding," Zane explained. "It's actually called Kinbaku, "the beauty of tight binding," and the goal is to create beauty as well as to give the bound person pleasure while their body is displayed." He clicked through some of his crazy-erotic photographs projected on the wall. "The pleasure is heightened by the knots and bindings placed strategically on erogenous zones to stimulate them."

Hmmm. Placing them strategically. I'll have to remember that. At that moment I saw Liz walking toward me, dressed from neck to toe in a black fishnet body stocking. Her face was also painted in a black fishnet pattern, her eyes made up in an exaggerated style, with false eyelashes. I knew it was her, though. Our time last Saturday was burned into my brain.

"Hey Liz," I said, not wanting to startle her when I stepped out of the shadows.

"Anthony!" She grabbed my my arm. "I'm glad you made it, I like your mask, very Zorro. How do I look?" She twirled around, showing me her fine ass and her long hair, braided in the back like all the shibari models on the internet. The pros attach the braid to the bindings, creating a little pleasure-pain tension on the scalp, but uuuhhh…I'd decided to leave that to the pros.

"Totally amazing," I said, holding her hand as we stepped out into the room, where all eyes immediately riveted on Liz.

Zane winked at us and said to the crowd, "John and Yoko here are beginners. John's been doing some research on the internet, just as you would do. He has a simple plan for tying Yoko up, and I'm going to do a more elaborate suspension on James here."

We chuckled at the John and Yoko pseudonym Zane gave us, and Liz (shorter in her bare feet) stood on tiptoe to whisper in my ear. "I can't believe you volunteered for this! Are you really a beginner?" She has the tendency to chatter when she's nervous, and she was definitely nervous. "I've always wanted to do this, and I'm so glad it's you."

Pulsing house music set the mood while Zane went to work, rapidly creating beautiful knots on James' chest, back and groin, while simultaneously creating a spider web of suspension from his arms and legs to the ceiling. James was wearing a skin-colored Speedo that did little to hide the fact that being tied up was turning him on.

While the focus was on James, I felt the need for a warm-up myself. Pulling Liz back into the hallway, I kissed her hard, hearing her gasp with surprise at my quick movements as I ran my hands over her body and then gripped her ass cheeks, pulling her into me.

"Are you ready for this?" I panted, my heart banging in my chest, and she nodded, her eyes wide but trusting. We were both vibrating with the intensity of this sexually charged atmosphere as we went back into the room, where Zane was giving more details about the art of Kinbaku while methodically tying and photographing his work. His subject, James, now seemed completely blissed out while he floated serenely on his suspension.

Showtime! Liz stood tall and relaxed, her arms up and elbows out, with fingertips touching the back of her neck, while I spoke quiet instructions to her. I started by winding red rope around her waist three times, making it snug but not uncomfortable. Asking her to spread her legs a little, I tucked the rope under the back of the waist cinch and ran it between her legs, up through the front of the waist and back again, the two red ropes highlighting the outer lips of her fishnet-covered labia.

Zane handed me a thin, knotted cord, instructing me privately to thread it through the fishnet in the back and tuck it under the waist rope. Then I pulled it tight through her slit and pushed it under the rope in front. The strategic knots he'd tied pressed directly on her anus and her clit, and Liz started fidgeting, twisting her hips to move the silk cord where it would create the most pleasure.

Her breasts looked so high and proud with her arms up like that, I wanted to bury my face between them, but…she said she'd always wanted to try this, saying, "I like being dirty with my lover in front of other people." Feeling like the luckiest bastard on earth, I took a new piece of rope and circled three times underneath her breasts and three times over the upper slopes of them, crossing the red rope in an X in the center, then winding the rope around and around and around each breast until they stood straight out from her chest in their red 'bra,' the areolae and her nipples fuller, larger and more erect than I had seen them up to now. In the background, we heard the camera, and the murmur of people talking just below the music, but we stayed focused on each other.

The effect of the black fishnet bound by the red rope was obscenely erotic, and Liz looked down, watching her breasts react to their bonds and humming under her breath, obviously trying hard not to moan while I whispered encouragement and gave her little kisses.

"What does it feel like?" I asked her, standing close.

"They feel…so heavy, I can feel my breasts throb," she said in a dreamy voice. "I feel those knots, those secret knots, and I want to come so bad, I feel myself wanting and clutching inside." The sound of her arousal shot straight to my cock, and my erection was close to painful. Little goose bumps rose under the fishnet, while her skin, and especially her breasts, flushed.

After she dropped her arms, I wrapped her elbows in the rope and attached them to her waist cinch. I looked at Zane, not wanting to leave her side, since she now couldn't catch herself if she lost her balance. Zane went behind Liz and supported her head on his shoulder while I lifted her feet, and we lowered her carefully into her rope cradle, where her entire body lay supported in a sensual display. Her whimpers and moans were a little louder now as I moved around her, touching her breasts and between her legs, kissing her, telling her how awesomely beautiful she was.

Zane handed me a pair of red ankle cuffs to raise and spread her legs and attach them to the ropes, but I hesitated, wondering if that last bit of lost mobility would scare her.

After studying her carefully, assessing her eyes and her body language, he said, "Do it. She's ready for it, and we're almost done here."

Zane was walking people out the door when I heard him say, "It might appear as if the submissive is being tortured, but they would tell you they feel comfortable, at peace, more free than they've ever felt before. For some people, it's the first time they can simply BE."

Damned if he wasn't right! Her legs suspended at a comfortable angle, she appeared to be in the ecstatic head space I read about in the blogs, her eyes fixed on me as she twisted and turned in her ropes in an uninhibited attempt to make herself come.

We were finally alone in the room, the lights lowered, and I unbound Liz's breasts and caressed them, bringing the circulation back fully as she brought herself to orgasm with a keening cry. Her sounds, her pleasure, were a revelation, along with the idea that I didn't have to hide how much this turned me on, and neither did she! Here was my darkest fantasy come to life, and she not only accepted it, she wanted to take it to the next level.

When the last wave of her orgasm rolled over her, I took the top of her body stocking in both hands and ripped it all the way down the center, her lush breasts spilling free and her wet pussy spread and open for me like a glistening flower. She was so hot, thrusting herself at me, asking me to fuck her in a husky, drunk-sounding voice. And the suspension was at exactly the right height for me to do it.

Instead I pulled over a stool and just sat, staring at her, touching her clit with my fingers, squeezing it, blowing on it until her juices were running. Her cries of passion filled the room when I used my mouth and tongue to make her come, one orgasm flowing into the endless next when I did it again. And then again, Liz coming hard and fast this time. She seemed suspended in her pleasure, totally consumed by the sensations I was giving her, letting me know she loved to come and wasn't afraid to ask for it with her hot sex noises.

Finally I stood, pulling my cock out, sheathing it and coming inside her, finding it easier than ever to hit the spot inside her that made her scream and come again as I pressed deep into her, pulling on the ropes around her waist so her breasts bounced with each thrust. God, that was hot! She stared into my eyes and I loved the sensation of the whole length of her pussy tightening around me, my vision going white when a shattering climax hit me.

I knew if it was me in those ropes, my adrenalin would be dropping and I would start to feel sore, so I pulled myself together quickly. When her legs were free, I put her feet on the ground and knelt between them, untying her arms and waist while rubbing and massaging every inch of her, including her scalp.

In the blogs they called this aftercare. She was whispering some of her feelings and observations to me, her voice hoarse from coming, then giggling and kissing me while she calmed from flying on her ropes.

By the time we finished, there was no one left in the club, so I put my shirt around her and walked her up to her office, where she dressed. We went to her place because it was closer, whispering in the dark and playing around. Friday extended into Saturday, and we went to an art museum in town, holding hands and remembering this and that about our experience. She kept thanking me for surprising her, like I did her a favor, which was totally ridiculous. I felt like I was sixteen again and falling hard without a net to catch me.

Chapter Seven

Anthony

MY SISTER WENDY is one of the most sensible people I know. And she's a shrink, so absolutely nothing anyone could say would shock her. When I found myself driving over to her house Sunday afternoon, I knew it was because I needed to talk with someone I could trust about my Liz Carleton situation.

Wendy's garage door was open when I drove up, and she was sitting in the middle of a big tarp, surrounded by pieces of stainless steel, grates, bolts, and screws that appeared to belong to the barbecue grill pictured on the front of the giant box behind her. The good news was she would have plenty of time to talk while we put this thing together. The bad news? Wendy hates reading instruction manuals.

The fact that she was actually reading said instructions was not a good sign. She usually ignores them and "goes with it." The big schematic spread out on the floor, and the way she was frowning and shaking her head meant she was already desperate. When she saw me, the look on her face was a cross between a person who sees an oasis in the desert and a kid offered candy.

A slow smile spread across her face while she looked me over, yesterday's stubbly beard and last night's clothes making it obvious I hadn't gone home last night. "Hey, bro, you're…just in time!"

"I can see that." I unfolded a lawn chair leaning against the wall, sat in it, and took the instruction book from her hands. "Where's Ally?" I asked, looking around for my eighteen-year-old niece.

With a big sigh, she gestured toward the driveway. "As you can see, there's no car. She has her driver's license now, did you know that, Uncle Anthony?"

I nodded without looking up from the instructions. "Actually, I did know that. And did you know there actually are places you can buy a grill and they'll put it together for you? What did you buy, the online special?" I knew she hated that preachy tone, but I couldn't resist. It's a big brother thing.

Wendy stuck her tongue out at me as if we were still schoolkids, waving a handful of screwdrivers. "Yes, I did! Not everyone is a rich, hotshot lawyer like you!"

I took the screwdrivers from her, and in no time we had the base put together, wheels and all.

Suddenly I was swamped with memories of when my daughters were new drivers. "I remember those days with my girls. They couldn't wait to get the hell out on the road." Then I started laughing. "I remember one time I went home for lunch on a weekday. When I came back out of the house, Lyndsey had taken my car, and I was due in court in an hour! Thank God for cell phones, but she actually talked me into letting her drop me off at the courthouse, knowing I could walk to my office from there."

We were both on our knees now, successfully lifting the grill onto the base, and Wendy crawled over and gave me a hug. "You taught her to negotiate, big guy, and see? That's one of the many things I love about you! You have this uptight, tough guy image, but you're a big softy underneath all that macho-ness."

Looking over my rumpled clothes again, she added, "And I can tell you went out last night, and you haven't been home yet. So who talked you into staying the night, Mr. Walk of Shame?"

Her question triggered images of Liz, her lips swollen from my kisses, her hands unbuckling my belt, her silky hair all over the pillow when I woke up this morning. The way she smiled when I brought her coffee and a cinnamon roll in bed. No shame in any of that.

"Uh, hellooo…earth to Anthony?" She slapped me on the back, laughing as she screwed the base on. "So tell me about the woman who put that dreamy look on your face."

Picking up the lid and placing the back over the proper holes, I managed to force the thoughts of Liz out of my mind. "She's…uh…someone I knew from Lucidcom. Liz Carleton."

Wendy never forgets a name or a face. "Liz Carleton. I'm sure I met her. Oh, yeah, at the house after…"

I raised my hand in warning, not wanting her to say "Serena's funeral" out loud. Unsure *why* I couldn't hear that right now, I was sure nonetheless.

My sister's initial glance was assessing, but she didn't look at me while we fastened the lid.

"I remember she is very attractive and smart," she mused once the lid was in place. "She had a boyfriend at the time, and he was there." When she met my eyes, her eyebrows were raised. "I assume he's out of the picture, huh? So how many times have you been out with Liz, and why haven't I heard about her? How about starting to fill me in now?"

Embarrassed by the answer, I fudged it a little. "The boyfriend is long gone, and we've been out twice." It was actually only last night, but I decided to count our La Vida legal consultation/outing as a "date." If I went to her right now, I thought, she'd open up to me, let me take her in my arms and…

Wendy stood straight, her hands on her hips, and landed a playful swat on my arm. "Oh, my God, look at you! You…you're blushing, actually blushing. You've just hooked up with her since you were at my house last week, haven't you?!"

Shaking her head, Wendy raised her eyebrows, eyes wide. "Isn't this a little sudden to be considered serious?" Her eyes narrowed, checking out my face. As a lawyer, I've cultivated a world-class poker face, but my little sister can see right through me. "She must be some kind of crazy sorceress, affecting Stone Cold Anthony like this!"

I held up my hand again, willing that ridiculous name to go away, not wanting to react to it, but shaking with laughter nonetheless. "Stone Cold Anthony!? Who the hell came up with that one?"

Turning away to pick up the grates and humming as she put them in the grill, she purred, "Your niece, Ally. She called you that for years, and said you were emotionally unavailable until recently, when you guys went fishing together. Now she's decided you're simply introverted."

As I screwed the handle on the lid, it was my turn to shake my head. "Holy shit, Wendy, you've got Ally talking the shrink talk already?" I rubbed my hand over my face, stalling, because I wasn't ready to describe this sudden crazy attraction I was feeling for Liz. *Describe* it? Hell, I wasn't even ready to accept the idea it *existed* yet.

When Serena was sick, and after she died, I had to step up from the second-string Dad role, and my life suddenly revolved around my girls, 16 and 20 at the time. They were often angry about the whole thing, and who could blame them? So was I.

During those years, Wendy was the sounding board for all of us. Now we were a few years into living life without Serena, we had officially banned that famous shrink question Wendy was always asking: "How does that make you feel?" We'd been through the birthdays, Mother's Days and Christmases without Serena, learning how to guard our hearts while still remembering her.

My daughters were now independent young women, and in the past six months, I'd begun to feel like I'd gotten my life back together, orderly and predictable. And then Liz happened.

Wendy and I hooked up the gas lines, and she was beaming because we'd managed to put the thing together without putting anything upside down or backwards. We had four pieces left over, some screws and a random shiny metal piece so, despite Wendy's protests, I did a ten-minute staredown about the metal triangle, stalking around the grill, mostly to avoid her demand for a description of my new relationship.

"Anthony, *stop*! It works, thank you, forget about that stupid piece!" Hooking her arm through mine, she dragged me inside. "I made some eggplant parm, come help me eat it." I was always a sucker for her eggplant (which comes from my garden, by the way), so I sat down at the breakfast bar in her kitchen, savoring the smell of roasted garlic and cheese filling the air.

She poured a glass of the homemade red wine I make every year in the fall, the kind Italians affectionately call 'dago red.' I grow hydroponic grapes in a greenhouse, and others outside at the back of my property, mix them with hybrids from Europe and California, and make a mellow red blend. It's totally different from commercial bottled wines, but delicious and, to me at least, oddly comforting. Probably because my dad (Anthony the Second) made it, and it felt so right for Anthony the Third to do the same.

After we'd eaten and poured a second glass, Wendy got quiet. One elbow on the bar, she leaned her head onto her hand and lifted her chin at me. "I know you want to run this by me, and that's why you came here. Start at the beginning, and tell me everything that happened. Well, maybe not *everything*…"

Sighing heavily, I sat back and gave in to my sister's eager questions. "My partner's assistant hired Carleton Public Relations to do social media for us, but I was surprised when Liz, the PR gal I knew from Lucidcom, made an appointment to see me. I assumed she would try to sell me on using more of her company's services, and I was certainly open to the idea.

"I was impressed with her when we worked together years ago. At Lucidcom, I enjoyed talking with her about work issues, because she was always very sharp. And I guess we were a little flirty with each other, in a friendly way. Nothing was ever inappropriate, and we liked each other.

"When she walked in last week, I was…well…Liz Carleton is one of the few women I've ever seen who's gotten better-looking as she got older. She's tall and extremely…stylish, and these days she's got kind of uuuhhh…sexy librarian thing going on." I paused, remembering how her heels were a little too high, making her hips sway when she walked. At times her glasses were perched on the end of her nose, then she hung them from the neck of her pink sweater, right between her…

"Uh-huh, yeah, keep going Romeo," Wendy said with a laugh. Apparently I'd paused for more than a few moments.

"She twists her hair into…I don't know, not a bun, but, smooth, like…" Making a motion with my hands, I pretended to roll a handful of hair sideways.

"A French twist, I think it's called." My sister was watching me, laughing to herself. "A very retro hipster kind of style, so she probably has long hair."

I guess imagining long hair and saying "French" when describing anything about Liz was a turn-on, since my trousers were getting tight. "I guess women know all about this stuff," I chuckled, and promptly got lost in a daydream again. I started to imagine myself taking Liz's hair down again, pin by pin, and running my fingers through it. *Whew, I've got it bad!*

She read my mind. "You have a thing for her, I guess."

"She invited me to a private club and…then we ended up at her place." I conveniently neglected to mention she *owns* the club, and we had sex in her office. Thank God Wendy didn't dig in to the private club thing, because that would have been awkward.

"She's funny and very straightforward, and we both have a shitload of baggage. She seems up for a good time, but not actually looking for a relationship. I mean, I only recently met her in this context and…I don't even know why I'm talking to you right now." I shook my head as she read my expression. "Put me out of my misery. What…what are you thinking?"

"I'm thinking I love hearing this from you, haven't heard it since, uh, you know. I think you're scared to let your emotions out of their cave, but I'm glad you *can* feel this way, aren't you?"

"Of course, but I mean, it's not like Serena."

"No, it's not, but that's good. You and Serena were kids, sixteen when you met."

"And it's not like I haven't been with women since…"

She held her hands up to her ears. "La, la, la, laaaaaah! I don't want to hear about my brother with random hookups, puhleeease!" Then she took a deep breath and added, "But the fact that you're telling me about Liz tells me this is different." I nodded. "Of course, you need to see where it goes. You can handle it."

I started getting my jacket and phone together and she gave me a big hug. "Thanks for helping me with the grill, bro. I'd still be sitting there praying for a miracle."

Before I walked out the door, she said, "Don't do your strategic lawyer thing with this one, Anthony. I know you, you like to let the other person make the first move so you know which way the wind is blowing, so you don't get caught unaware. Let her know how you feel sooner rather than later, okay? In honor of Mom, I'm going to say a little prayer to Saint Anthony to protect your tender little heart."

"Is this where the violins start playing, sis?" I gave her a peck on the cheek and headed out the door, feeling like a man on a mission. My mother had a special saying about Saint Anthony, "Saint Anthony, please look around; something is lost and must be found." In this case, maybe he needed to help me find the part of me that died with my wife.

Chapter Eight

Liz

A S SOON AS Anthony answered the door, I realized I was overdressed.

Instead of the usual beautiful slacks and white shirt, he had on a faded work shirt and a snug pair of jeans so worn they knew him by name. "Oh, sorry," he said, scrubbing his hand down his unshaven face. "I said wear jeans, I thought that would cover it. Sorry, should've been more specific. I forgot to tell you I'm kind of a gentleman farmer, so, uh, we're spending the day at a farm."

My $180, strategically ripped skinny jeans and high heels did not fit his super-casual look.

"You do look hot, though," he grinned.

Already a bit breathless because I loved the way he looked in his jeans, I was willing to overlook the fact that he was acting a little cranky.

"Yeah…uh, I have some sneakers in the car, let me go get them." Truth be told, I'd packed a little overnight bag 'cause I was hoping for another marathon weekend with him.

"Bring the heels back with you though, okay? You can put those back on later."

"Pretty sure of yourself, aren't you?" I smirked.

"Should I *not* be?" he threw back, giving me the silly Groucho eyebrows. "Don't you think I *know* you're just using me for sex?!"

He does have very defined, dark eyebrows. They are probably the only part of his face that gives him away, knit together when he's concerned, high and wide when he's surprised. The brows were in neutral when I got back to the porch, a folder and my high heels in my hands. *Confident bastard.*

He'd texted me during the week: *I'm taking Friday off. Come to my place? Off Russel St in Red Rock.* Typical male text, right? "Here's the info. Mission complete. Over and out."

I texted back, but he called last night, late-ish. Predictably, the conversation wandered into sexty "What are you wearing right now?" territory. Coming from him, talking about sexy times on the phone was hot. From anyone else, it would be sketchy at best. Yes, he told me to "just wear jeans."

Rocking on his porch swing, we drank a lovely, mellow red. "We both live in kind of unconventional homes, don't we?" I said, enjoying the desert-style landscaping and the pine trees surrounding his house and…barn? "It's peaceful. I've never seen this part of Red Rock, and I've lived here all my life." He seemed zoned out, and I was doing all the talking. I knew I could get his attention by putting my hand on his thigh though, so I did.

He put his hand on mine and shook his head. "I seem to be saying I'm sorry a lot. It's only…do you have public relations clients you wish you didn't have?"

"Are you kidding me?! About half of them drive us all insane with irrational expectations!"

"This was a week from hell. I thought about you a lot

when I wanted to escape." Tilting his head back, he drained his glass to the bottom. "I like that we turn our phones off when we're together. I never thought about doing that until you suggested it."

"Hey, we're both self-employed, so in our minds, we're always working. At least this way, people can learn to solve a few problems without us, right? Speaking of which..." I handed him the folder from my car. "I didn't have a chance to scan this in. It's the latest chapter in the harassment situation I emailed you about."

"Oh, yeah, that lawyer couple seems bent on torturing you...the Morrows, isn't it?"

I nodded.

"I asked around about them at the courthouse," he continued, "and everyone, and I mean universally *everyone*, detests Jane and Keith Morrows. According to the police report, there's no evidence you or anyone from the club spray-painted their truck. The business owners they interviewed at your office park seem to love you because you save them money, filling the potholes and resurfacing the parking lot all the time."

Surprised and pleased he'd already looked into it, I gave him a peck on the cheek. "Yes, I do that," I said, forcing a smile. "In the file is a restraining order they just filed against me, claiming I've been threatening and stalking them. And a civil suit, claiming I've caused them all kinds of mental anguish. Can you imagine?! Now I can't even go over and try to resolve this in person." Shaking my head, I added, "There's nothing to be done about the crazies! Let's stop talking about them, please. Tell me about your crazies instead, okay?"

"Sure, and believe me, I have them too. Everybody does. I'm starting to understand why people become scientists and software developers, so they only have to interact with test tubes and keyboards. When Leah's out of school, I'm going to start pruning my client list and get rid of the annoying, shady people. I seem to attract a higher percentage of those types because of being Italian, ya' know?" He made a funny, twisted-up face and put on an Italian accent. "Dey tink I'm connected, ya' know what I mean?" He shrugged. "But I'm not."

I'd almost forgotten one of the things that attracted me to Anthony back when we worked for the same company—other than the fact that he's tall, dark and handsome—was the fact that he's so funny.

"I've been putting money aside," he continued, "and I want to cut back overall, enjoy life more." He put his hand on my thigh now, his big palm moving in circles. "I have extra money and time to spend on myself now, with Leah almost finished with school. How about you? Are you getting more focused on building your empire?"

His words should've stuck an icicle in my heart, but they didn't. Suddenly I wanted nothing more than to be part of his vision. We were almost the same age, but miles apart in where we were in the timelines of our lives. I felt like telling him I didn't give a shit about building my empire, but instead I said, "Enjoying life sounds good. I have big plans for that."

I have to tell him, I have to tell him was the refrain in my head, but instead, I changed the subject, chattering away.

"You have to tell me about this crazy-looking Jeep," I said, indicating the vehicle parked next to mine, which looked like an escapee from a monster truck rally. "Is it really yours?"

He nodded.

"It is so incredibly…sexy! It looks like something from a movie set." Black on black, without a sliver of chrome showing, the doors were off, and there were no windows or roof of any kind, just a truly filthy front windshield, and some giant, gnarly tires, and extruded mirrors spattered with mud. "This is the kind of car I'd expect Deadpool or Jason Bourne to drive."

"I use it to cart stuff around my little vineyard here. Since you're drinking my wine, do you want a tour?"

"Of course!" I jumped up and put my hand in his and squeezed. "Anthony Anzione, you are *such* a renaissance man!" It was a big step up to the Jeep's seat, so I was glad for the sneakers. "A vineyard! Aaayy, now *that's* Italian!"

He laughed at my sad excuse for an Italian accent and fired up the noisy vehicle. He often seems a little flat (like he had been when I arrived) when I first see him, and then brightens when we're together for a while. Digging into the seat crack, I found an old lap belt and fastened it, since there was no evidence of any other restraint.

Men like Anthony usually need to build something with their hands. and this impressive little vineyard was clearly Anthony's "something." Maybe guys like him do it because they're good at it, or maybe it's simply the way they're wired. I'd already seen (and benefitted from) the way Anthony had to touch everything, though in the office he was as hands-off as the next guy, giving the handshakes and sideways hugs appropriate for a sterile office environment. Of course he always *talked* with his hands, but everyone wrote that off as his Italian heritage.

"The barn was here when I bought the place, but I did all this." Inside the barn, he gestured at the rows of grow lights and grapes growing hydroponically. "These plants, and the ones outside, they're all hybrids, Italian-American, and I take them somewhere else to actually press and make the wine." He paused and narrowed his eyes at me. "Hey, am I boring the crap out of you, City Girl?"

"No! Absolutely not," I answered. "I am interested in this

side of you, Nature Boy!" Me, walking around in a vineyard? Nothing about it made any sense at all, but I was enjoying the hell out of it anyway.

We drove to the very end of the property, and he showed me how he built the trellises and attached the vines to them and installed the intricate irrigation system. "I started this right after…right after Serena, and the girls liked coming out here, too. Staying in the old house was…we moved out here full time two years ago. Of course, now they both have their own places."

My heart ached for him, losing Serena, and then, in a sense, losing his daughters to their bright futures. One loss was unexpected and unfair, the other a normal part of life, but that didn't make either of them any less of a loss.

He seemed upset after that, but as we talked and walked along the rows, he was fixing things, touching the plants, pulling things off them, and sending me back and forth to get gadgets from the Jeep. While filling a basket with the gorgeous eggplants and peppers growing near the vines, I caught up with him, handing him some kind of fancy tool. "You healed yourself doing all this," I said. "You should be very proud of yourself."

"Thank you," he replied, nodding. "I think that may be true." His fingers were bruised, and his arms scratched from the vines, but he seemed to revive while we moved down the long rows of plants stretching toward the rangy pines surrounding the property. "Like many Italians, I grow vegetables too. We have a complicated history with our gardens. Back in the old days, we used to grow stuff in secret, hide it from our enemies, because good food is so important to us."

"I get that. Are you making eggplant for dinner?" He shrugged, nodding and laughing. "I love eggplant almost as much as ravioli," I continued. "I went to Italy a few years ago with my mom and sisters, and I crave the food." I smiled at the memory. "We ate and drank like queens! We stayed in a bed and breakfast, and they made everything from their garden. The vegetables tasted so fresh and real, the sauce homemade. And the ravioli! To die for! Unbelievable!"

"Ha! I took the girls, and we did the same thing. Italians just seem to know how to live well."

Anthony wore a Phillies cap, and had this boyish way of pushing the brim back when he was thinking, wiping the sweat off his forehead with the back of his hand.

"Hey, my brother Cole is a big Phillies fan. You too?"

"Yeah, my dad was a fan." Anthony took off his hat and put it back on, his hair all crazy underneath.

"What is it about the Phillies? Why are the fans are so passionate? I read somewhere the games sell out whether they win or lose."

"I think it's like the saint I'm named after, St. Anthony. He's the saint of lost causes and lost items, and Phillies fans are apparently into lost causes as well. I know my dad was. He was always going broke betting on race horses. Maybe you've heard the jokes about the Phillies...what do you call a Phillies fan with a World Series ring? A thief! I mean, 1980 and 2008 had to have been flukes!"

I told him about a long-ago good memory of my dad and I growing tomatoes in our backyard when we were stationed in Germany. "The other kids don't remember this at all. Actually, they don't remember Dad before the booze. He lost a buddy in some stupid friendly fire incident in Yemen in 1986. After that it was the two A's—alcohol and affairs. He was an alcoholic and he...was not a bad person, but he was emotionally unavailable. Reacting to his affair, my mother taught me not to trust men."

I took a deep breath, then let it out with a whoosh. "There. My truth is right there for you. Mom was critical, and had high expectations of me, treating me like a partner in raising the other kids, the person she could rely on as they came along. I rose to the occasion, no coddling for me!

"But I craved it, I wanted someone to care for me. When Ethan and I got together, it felt like caring. And when I hit my thirties, I saw couples who seemed to trust each other, like you and Serena."

He gave me a back rub, as if sensing how much it cost me to bring up Serena, how I feared being compared with her. "Family, right? My dad was a compulsive gambler, which is why I had to go into the service to go to college. But I have fond memories of the Phillies games." Pulling off his beloved cap, Anthony showed me the sweat-stained hatband. "Ten years, and I've never washed it—how would I do that?"

"Wait…Never!?" I snatched my hand away from that hat like it was on fire.

Anthony's laugh was like the best book you ever read, the kind you didn't want to end. "Ha! I wash it all the time and dry it stretched on a rock in the sun. Psych!" He grabbed the basket and put his tools in there with the veggies.

For a while we just walked hand in hand, circling back around toward the Jeep, and soon hand-holding turned into kissing. He pulled me against him, his skin warm from the sun as he ravished my mouth. We made out like teenagers on a bench under a tree until I thought I would lose my mind.

He feverishly unzipped my pants and slid his fingers to the edge of my panties, sliding against my clit. Anthony was good at coming up with innovative techniques to pleasure my pussy with those callused fingers of his, learning every little angle to torture me, inside and out. Delicious, delicious torture.

He pushed my shirt up and pulled my tits over the top of my sports bra, squeezing the nipples close together and ready for his mouth. Anthony Anzione was always so confident, and he knew how to use that confident mouth of his. I arched my back into him, desperate for his lips. Alternating pinching one nipple and sucking the other, he made me squirm and reach into his jeans, but he moved away, peering up at me slyly so I could get a good look at his wet lips latched onto my breast.

After all the breast play and tuning me up with his fingers in my cunt, I was writhing on that bench like a sinner in hell.

Then he did the unthinkable. He twisted one nipple tight with his fingers and bit down on the other one! That did it. My orgasm was a screamer—so what if I was outdoors where anyone could hear me? He held me and kissed me, stroking my hair, while I calmed.

Taking off his shirt and covering me with it, he massaged my shoulders and told me to hang out for a minute and then meet him over at the Jeep.

When I got there, he had cleared some things off, and was sitting in the back seat, flashing me a mischievous grin and patting his lap, signaling me to sit there. He took off his shirt, unfastened his slacks and shoved them down, freeing his erection. "C'mere Liz. Come sit on my lap, baby, but take your clothes off first. All the way off this time."

"Don't you want to, uh…" I pointed in the general direction of his house, but he slowly shook his head and crooked a finger at me. I plopped my clothes on the driver's seat and climbed aboard, straddling him while he rolled on a condom. He reached for my hand and nipped the fleshy part of my thumb, making me shiver.

How to please me, how to touch me…Anthony seemed to intuitively know exactly how to do it. His focus on my pleasure made me forget all about my business and my quest for the perfect Viking baby.

He was holding my waist while I lowered myself on his cock, when he said, "You see the roll bar above you? Put your hands on it."

Oooo, I can raise and lower myself using this bar, so hot. I started circling my hips, taking deep breaths as I felt myself stretch around him. Anthony gave me permission to be bad—not that I needed it, but he was so good at taking it to filthy new levels I would never have thought of on my own.

"Your tits look fantastic like this," he said, stroking them with those long fingers of his, making my nipples even tighter. When he cupped my breasts and put his mouth on first one, then the other, stroking his beard across sensitive skin on the way from one to the other, my head fell back, and I stopped caring if someone might be watching us. In fact, it turned me on to think they might!

Reading my mind, he said, "You'd like it if someone was watching, wouldn't you, you dirty girl? Don't close your eyes, look at me, because you're gonna come real quick, and so am I. Grind me, Liz, c'mon, grind me."

My heart pounded as I was moving up and down, then circling, so my clit got extra attention. His hands on my waist kept the rhythm as he thrust up and met me while I hung onto the roll bar for leverage. Hitting my swollen bud with every move, he stayed with me as I convulsed around him, filling the air with my cries. His final lunge into me was a straining motion, an explosion of pleasure as he shook with a massive orgasm.

He finally closed his eyes, breaking our erotic staredown. When we were both calm, he wondered aloud, "Mmmm, how many times can I make that happen?"

I didn't have an answer. The thing we had freed something wild in me that had been hidden in a dusty, neglected corner. I stayed there on his lap, facing him, playing with his beard and his hair and kind of hanging out naked in his ridiculously macho Jeep. "I think we should explore how many times you can make it happen over the entire weekend. What time is dinner?"

Chapter Nine

Liz

UNCONCERNED THAT HE was naked, Anthony got out of bed the next morning and picked up my clothes along with his, folding them neatly on the dresser. He didn't know I was watching him in his messy yet adorable state. He was such a gorgeous man, dark and powerfully masculine, the formidable muscles in his back and legs flexing while he moved around the room.

Men like Anthony must be used to people looking at them, whether they're standing up in a courtroom or pushing a shopping cart in the grocery store. In addition to being the tallest and fittest man in almost any room, he was also a sharp dresser. I knew *I'd* be thinking about him every ten minutes at work again, the broad shoulders and the long legs, the sexy kisses. And those perky buns of steel, dear God! The man does not skimp on the squats, it's plain to see!

But it was more than his looks. I felt an electric charge when I was in his presence; he seemed to command the space around him. Even years ago when we worked together, I always noticed how he dominated any room he walked into, assuming leadership without even trying.

The morning sun lit the touch of silver in his wavy black hair, only making him look sexier, and his strong features would have inspired Michelangelo to get out the sculpting tools. The lines at the corners of those intense brown eyes merely proved he smiled and laughed a lot, unusual for a guy as formidable as he is.

Now I thought about it, he generally seemed more relaxed than he had back in the day. He was smiling right now, drawing attention to his irresistible, full lips. And really, that smile was his secret weapon, fooling opponents who didn't realize he was about to shred any opposition to whatever he was proposing. It was a fatal mistake to think smiling Anthony Anzione was Mr. Nice Guy instead of the shrewd operator he truly was.

But right now he was *actually* nice, so carefree he seemed like a different person. Maybe super-hot sex had that effect on him?!

"Would you like to meet for lunch next week?" he asked, throwing himself on the bed and propping his head on one elbow. "One of my daughters, Leah, is interning this summer, going back to Penn soon, and you could meet her. The three of us can go to one of my favorite places, right near the office. They have the best homemade ravioli!

I paused a minute, and I'm sure my eyes betrayed my shock. He's talking about lunch? And meeting his daughter? I forced my face to smile. "Of course! I'm surprised you...you know...remembered about the ravioli. Uh...how much I like them."

He pulled me close, his dick hard again against my belly, but he was shaking with laughter. One hand twined in my hair, he leaned away, forcing me to look in his eyes. "You are *not*! You're not surprised about the ravioli! You should've seen your face just now."

Pulling me in tight for a full-body hug, he spoke softly into my ear. "You're surprised I'm inviting you to meet my daughter in the daylight, in front of people we might know." He exhaled, then buried his face in my hair. "Why, Liz, why?! Did you think I was going to keep you on the side…that you'd be my dirty little secret?!"

Busted! Besides being an amazing hunk of man meat, Anthony was extremely good at reading my mind, in the bed and out of it. Minutes ago, I was drowning in those brown eyes of his. Then tears threatened to fill my eyes—*tears*, goddamn it—and all I could do was nod.

"Liz, you're…what, almost forty? I'm forty-five! We don't play games like that, we're too old. It amazes me you even think it!" He sat up, legs over the side of the bed, and pulled me onto his lap, into his chest. "The women in my office have been asking about you since the day you marched in there. They said I have a spring in my step for the first time since…for a while. They've asked a million questions about you." He waggled his eyebrows at me. "They've all been bugging me to start dating. My daughters, too."

I laughed. "Is that what we're doing, dating?"

Tracing a finger all around my lips, his voice was low and sexy. "Yeeess, we are doing the very best kind of dating, the kind that ends with a bang. So to speak." He was thoughtful for a moment, then rubbed his silky, bearded cheek on my chin. "Why do you ask? Do we need to do more dating and less…"

"Less banging?" I asked, and we both cracked up. "No, I think we have the perfect balance between banging and dating." I pressed into him, snuggling. "So they've been bugging you to date. How long has it been?"

He pulled a sheet off the bed and wrapped it around us. "I'm not a hookup kind of guy, but they've been trying to introduce me to everyone's mom, co-worker, sister, and whatever. It was awkward, and I usually didn't follow through. I did a little klutzy internet dating and I, uh, *was* seeing someone until a few months ago."

"So why are they bugging you to start dating?"

"I couldn't call what Nora and I did dating, I called it 'a business trip.' She was the one who said it was just sex. I flew to see her, or we met halfway since she lived in New York. It was a distance thing."

"OOOOhhhh, so she *wanted* to be the side chick?"

"That's what she said. She's an attorney, and we met at a conference last year. After about a year, she told me she didn't care for my...aggression was the word she used. It was confusing. We had vanilla sex, too, but she acted like she wanted to explore submission, like she enjoyed it, but...I guess not."

Huh. *Her loss, my rising orgasm count.* I turned to him, smiling at his obvious confusion. "Anthony, it's not you. I can tell you what the problem was, I think."

I lay back on the pillow and stared at the ceiling. This topic was something I'd thought about often over the years, but recently I'd been keeping a journal, writing about it, more to explain it to myself than anyone else. "Women are very confused when they discover submission turns them on. It's not what our culture teaches, and it seems to conflict with the whole 'I am woman, hear me roar' thing.

"Or, as one of my professors said, it clashes with the feminist worldview. *Fifty Shades of Grey* got people talking about it, but the dom in the book was messed up, the sub a naïve virgin. Your friend the lawyer probably felt there was something wrong with her, like she was acting out some sick psychological problem from her youth."

"And you? What do you think, Liz?" He was leaning in to

me, those warm brown eyes of his focusing intensely. He looked yummy all the time, but right now those melted chocolate eyes of his made me want to lick him from head to toe.

"I've struggled with it, gotta be honest," I told him. "I think men buy into the dysfunctional idea, too, the idea that you might have daddy issues or self-image issues or whatever. Of course, many people believe that about any woman who is highly sexual, that there's something wrong with her, like she's compensating for something she's lacking."

I sighed and stretched my arms up over my head, getting in a good cat stretch. "Looking back, I believe two of the men I dated over the years believed our relationship would never go anywhere serious because of my sexuality. Too freaky, I guess? They both turned around after our relationship and married younger women from…uh…sheltered backgrounds."

A lesser man would try to smooth things over and tell me I was imagining things, but Anthony was quiet, giving my words some serious thought. "Some men are threatened by you, I've noticed that. Some at the club, for sure, the ones who aren't sure of themselves, or are immature. And back when we were working together, people were intimidated by your confidence, I remember. But you still didn't answer my question. What does your submissive nature mean, in your mind?"

I had written in my journal about this but NEVER said any of it out loud. Sitting up straight, my hands pressed against my thighs, I took a deep breath. "First of all, it doesn't *define* me in any way. It's like saying a person is defined by their hobbies or their taste in movies. For me, it's nothing more than something I like to play around with during sex."

"I'm the same," he said, now moving his hand around my body under the sheet. "I felt myself, at one point, thinking about domination all the time. Maybe it was a metaphor for wanting to control things in my life, I don't know. I wanted to tie and bind and slap...all the time, like...I needed it. Then...life happened."

There was no need to get specific; we both knew what happened to teach him, in a brutal and definitive manner, that controlling your life is an illusion. The light came back in his eyes, and he said, "Now I feel like you do, it's a spicy and interesting option." Placing my hands up over my head, he held both my wrists in one hand and started planting kisses and stroking that beard on my face, neck and chest. "A very sexy, tempting option. But getting back to the other question, why are you like this? Who treated you like you're the side chick?"

"It was Ethan," I said, and Anthony rolled his eyes. "Ethan's the one who introduced me to the lifestyle. But I gotta say, before him, sex felt like something that happened *to* me, and I always wondered if there was more. I had all these preconceived notions about what sex should be or what I *should* like. But the first time we had sex, he told me he was into kink, and he could tell I would be too."

I tried not to notice the way Anthony tensed up and pulled away from me, his hands curled into fists. What guy wants to hear good things about another lover, particularly another dominant? Yet his eyes willed me to continue, assuring me he was okay with the discussion.

"Submitting to Ethan was a negotiation right from the start, figuring out *together* what I wanted to do and what my boundaries were, and I found it very...empowering. From that perspective, the number one thing I learned from the whole dom/sub experience is choice, that I can choose to surrender power for my own pleasure. I learned to try things and to trust my own body. Before him, no one asked what turned me on. Our scenes scared me, and it was exciting and raw, but I loved it!" I paused, knowing this was hard for Anthony. Stroking my arm with his hand, he nodded, signaling me to continue.

"Ethan turned out to be a cheating asshole, but as a dominant he was very mindful. I felt cared for, after years of caring for everyone else and being in charge for so many years…in fact, it's probably why my feelings for him blew up out of proportion. It ended after about three years, when he was on a business trip to Los Angeles. I surprised him, showing up at his hotel room and…when he opened the door, a woman called to him from inside the room, you know, 'Ethan, who is it?'"

Anthony shook his head and pulled me closer. "It turned out that the girl Ethan was fucking was wearing his ring, and they were engaged. Yeah, I actually *was* the side chick, the woman he was banging at the office. After that and then…Serena's funeral, I left and started my own company."

"I remember when you left. Right after…you know. That kicked my ass a little, and when I felt strong enough, I, too, left and started my firm. I owe you a thank-you for being my inspiration."

I noticed Anthony seemed to shift, to sit up straighter, and I paused. "Are you sure you want to hear all this shit? Maybe we should parse this out and talk about the rest of it some other time. Or never, eh?"

"Nope," he said, "let's do it." It's hard to describe how much I appreciated that he cared enough about me to hear everything. My useless ex would have found a way to blame me for what happened.

I cleared my throat, self-conscious about my rotten choices. "So I, uh, learned from that. I had a detective check out the other two long-term relationships I had over the years. They didn't cheat on me but…well, here I am, alone and forty. There was this guy…"

I had no idea why I was launching into all this crap with him. No one knew all of it, not even Lilly. This talking we were doing, it…showed me the control I thought I had over my life was fake, a fairy tale I told myself and the rest of the world.

"His name was Mark, and I met him through Lilly. He was a client of hers at the casino. He had such charisma, it was a high, and I felt lucky just being with him, and ignored the fact that he was isolating me from my friends and family. I was so dumb, I thought maybe we only needed each other and it was 'true love.' At some point he started saying critical things like 'You're not sexy when you cry, maybe you need to take something,' and 'An open relationship is part of the lifestyle.' We belonged to a club, which is part of why I later took over La Vida. I could see that many couples were exclusive."

I got out of bed and pulled on a robe, walking back and forth and gesturing. "Do you mind if I pace?"

Anthony skootched back against the headboard, his hair all messy and adorable. "Keep going. You're on a roll, Liz."

"Anyway…I denied Mark's subtle manipulation and controlling behavior because I was afraid to end the magic. When he started getting drunk and high all the time, he used gifts and trips to keep my hopes alive, but finally, finally…I ended it.

"It ended up happening at the perfect time for me, because my brothers were in Vegas on four months' leave. I spent a lot of time with them, and felt like a curtain had been lifted. I stopped answering Mark's calls when I realized I had to change, because he wasn't going to." Folding my arms across my chest, I stopped again and looked over at him. "Keep going or move on?"

He laughed and waved a "carry on" motion.

"I actually went on Match and met Martin, the nicest guy in the world. It was with him I finally got a glimpse of what it was like to be normal. I remember I backed his car up and rubbed up against a pole. When I told him about it, I was freaked, wondering if our relationship was over. Mark used to get so angry about things like that. Martin shrugged, got some stuff from his workshop, rubbed off the paint, and told me it was no big deal." I couldn't stop my voice from trembling when I said, "We were together for six months when I got a call from an unfamiliar number. It was his brother. He'd seen my number in his brother's phone. Martin had been killed in a car accident.

"So you can see I haven't been…uh…lucky in the relationship department. Ethan the cheater, Mark the manipulator, and Martin the nice guy. Those are my three to your wonderful one." Anthony held out his arms to me, and I crawled into them, enjoying the way he stroked my hair and kissed the top of my head. "So right now I'm seeing this guy who's very intense and sensual, you know? Also very smart and funny."

"He sounds fantastic," Anthony chuckled. "I hear he can cook, too!"

"Yes, he can. Did I mention he tends to be bossy?"

"Do tell?" he replied, one eyebrow raised.

Standing and taking off my robe, I decided I needed to be naked outside again. I'd just discovered that about myself. "The first one to the barn gets to be in charge," I yelled back at him as I ran out of the room. I *might* have let him get there first.

Chapter Ten

I GOT A text from Anthony on Wednesday. *Dinner tomorrow?* It told me a lot that he wanted to see me during the week after our intense three-day weekend. Of course, I was fighting to NOT think about him every ten minutes, but I also wondered if it was mutual. Weirdly, I think the fact that baby Lars was in the back of my mind made me braver, less anxious about how this would turn out. In at least one aspect of my future, I was already moving forward.

After years of dating, I kinda expected the worst. So many weird things happened. After a personal disclosure/porn star weekend like that, a guy might vanish into thin air, but Anthony obviously was ready to pick up where we left off.

My mind kept wandering back to when he sat on that stool and devoured my pussy while I was suspended on those ropes, so clearly enjoying what he was doing while I saw stars behind my eyelids. I squirmed in my desk chair. Whew! The man has some hot, raw skills!

Was it the intimate talk, or the other part he was craving? Hopefully both. I loved that he was thinking about me and making plans. I love a man with a plan when it involves…well, me!

Do you make a white wine? I texted. *I'll order in Chinese. 8?* Giggling at the way I was copying his texting style, I had to add a little winky face ;-). I avoid restaurants on work nights, since I'm almost always too tired for the waiting around part.

Sounds good. I'll bring wine.

The delivery guy was leaving when Anthony bounded up the steps, carrying flowers and a bottle of wine. We were both still dressed from work. "Flowers!" I squeaked, throwing my arms around his neck. "Hydrangeas! Where did you find those at this time of year?"

The smirky smile on his face told me his assistant bought them, but I'm okay with that. I do the same thing. "Thank you, you are so thoughtful." I said, arranging them in a vase.

We ate our Chinese and drank wine at the kitchen island, feeding each other with chopsticks. He started it. "Are you familiar with the word *umami*?" he said, dipping a chunk of lobster into some soy sauce and putting it in my mouth. "It kind of means savory things, things like soy sauce, that kick up flavor. So…sour, bitter, salty, sweet, *umami*."

"I have heard the term, but thought it was more foodie bullshit. When you say it, it might make sense. Or *maybe* all you're doing is teaching me to open my mouth when you want me to." When I said that, I opened my mouth wide and kind of waved my tongue at him.

Anthony cracked up and put another delicious bite in there. "Gotta admit, it sounds like an excellent strategy!" Licking his lips, he looked at me under those eyelashes of his and said, "You taste very *umami*, by the way."

"Well you taste *umami*, too," I said, clicking my chopsticks together so he would open his mouth wide.

Then I put a big old chunk of bok choy slathered with super-hot mustard in his mouth. Jumping off the kitchen stool, I raced out of the kitchen, and hearing him spit it out made me race faster. Seconds later he tackled me onto the couch, kissing me so deeply my mouth was thoroughly coated with hot mustard. Tears leaked from my eyes, but whether they were from the mustard or from laughing so hard, I wasn't sure.

When he sat straight and flipped me ass-up over his lap, pulling my skirt up at the same time, I knew I might be in some spicy trouble. He just sat there, not touching me. I pretended to ignore him, but that's hard to do when a man is staring at your ass and driving you nuts. Eventually he leaned over and kissed me, hot breath and feathery beard strokes heating up a spot on my back right above my butt. Goosebumps rose there and everywhere as I felt his fingers playing lightly over my skin and my panties. Then he ran his hand over me, fingers flat. I felt the heat of him through the thin panties and squirmed, anticipating a swat. *Wanting* a swat.

Waiting, waiting. Nothing. "You are mean," I said, looking over my shoulder at him.

"Not yet," he said, an evil smile on his face. "I want to see how long I can tease you. I want to hear you beg for me to be mean." He trailed his fingertips along the edge of my panties, grazing the skin underneath, light as a feather. He seemed pleased with my gasps and whimpers, his smile widening when I looked at him from under my hair. Pulling the crotch tight, he sawed the panties back and forth on my pussy a little, his fingers teasing the backs of my thighs now.

"Damn, man, can't you just…take off my panties?"

"Oh, yeah, I could. But I don't hear begging yet." He leaned back, his voice low and a little desperate when he added, "You look so hot, and I like your sexy wiggling. Let me help you out here." I felt cool air when he pulled the panties below the curve of my butt.

"Puhlllleeease," I whimpered. Was that enough begging? *SLAP!*

The sting was square in the center of one cheek, and I could feel every red fingerprint. He circled his hand there, the warmth of his palm both soothing and exciting me. "Spread your legs," he said, dipping a finger in and finding me wet and ready. "The way you respond to this...so amazing. Did you know you're lifting your ass up, that you want more?"

Honestly? I had no idea.

Landing a series of light slaps on both cheeks with the front and back of his hand made me feel tingly and turned on, and I wrapped my arms around his lower leg, digging my nails into the calves hiding under his dress slacks. I felt myself melting into him as he trailed his fingertips over my clit after each slap, making me twitch and moan while the swats got harder. "The last five are going to be tough," he said, "Count up from one, Liz!"

"One!" *Whack!* I *hate* counting spanks!

"Two!" *Whack!* Now Anthony was squirming and I felt his erection next to my belly.

"Threeeeeuuuuhhhh!" *Whack!* I couldn't help rocking against him, squeezing my legs together to relieve the need there.

"Four! MmmmmUhhhh..." *Whack!* I wailed in frustration, his sharp intake of breath telling me how turned on he was, by the feel, the sounds, the sight of us.

"Five!" *Whack!* Suddenly I *loved* counting spanks, because it was over, and he was stroking me reverently, groaning while he enjoyed the heat exchange, his palm to my ass.

His palm was still there somehow when he lifted me, carrying me to my bedroom as if I weighed nothing. I love the feeling of being different from him, his hard to my soft. Surprised when he deposited me in front of my full-length mirror, I was impressed when he showed me my behind in the mirror, tracing the red patterns slowly with his whole hand.

"Bend over and put your hands on the dresser," he commanded in a gruff voice, coming up behind me so we could both turn our heads and look in the mirror to the side. Or *I* could, actually. His eyes were glued to the red marks on my butt as he rolled on a condom, put both spread hands on my hips, and entered me in one swift thrust. I pressed back and he pushed forward at the same moment, triggering something inside me that made me gasp and bite my lower lip.

We got a sexy rhythm going, thrusting, circling and grinding into each other. Anthony leaned over and put his hands on my breasts, capturing the nipples between a thumb and forefinger as he drove into me, his thighs slapping against my ass. "Let's go Liz, let's come together and watch it in the mirror," he grunted, his voice husky with exertion. Crushing both my breasts into one hand, he reached down and squeezed my clit, holding me with his elbows tight to my sides as my pussy clenched around him and we both cried out, the erotic view in the mirror taking us to the next level and straight over.

Eventually we found my bed and he snuggled up behind me, kissing my shoulder and twining our legs together. For some reason, he then felt it was necessary to tickle me until I jumped up and stumbled into the shower. He shampooed and massaged my scalp and other body parts, and I gave him a blow job he will not soon forget, the streaming water washing away the cum I made him jack onto my breasts. I *loved* making him hot and watching him do that! While his legs were still trembling, I looked up at him and asked, "Moving on?"

Laughing and falling into bed, he mumbled, "I'll pick up my shirts on the way to the office and change so I don't look like Mr. Walk of Shame. Does that work?"

I took his face in both my hands and kissed him, then spooned into him, rubbing my red-hot butt against his dick. "I would love it. Would you make me breakfast?" He didn't answer because he was already asleep.

Chapter Eleven

FTER WORK ON the fifteenth day after my intimate three-way with Lars and my doctor, I felt the nasty, crampy feeling you get when you have your period. A trip to the bathroom confirmed that yes, it was leak week, shark week, and the floodgates of the red river were open. I guess I wasn't going to be needing a pregnancy test, so I texted Lilly: *Lars did not meet his true love this month.*

Later that evening my car was moseying over to my mom's house, the family home where I'd wiped so many snotty noses and watched while hundreds of birthday candles were blown out. Mom would be in bed, I knew, but it would be comforting to sleep in my childhood bedroom and wake up to talk to her before we both left for work. It felt like a good time to tell her about my plan to conceive a child (and how, so far, it wasn't working out).

Walking around to use the back door so I wouldn't wake her, I heard…sounds. A gasp, a moan, a man's low voice, the water splashing and bubbling in the hot tub on the back deck. The unmistakable sounds of passion. WTF?! A motion detector light switched on, shining in my face and mercifully blinding me from seeing my mother as she shrieked, "Oh my God, Liz!"

"Oh my God, Mom!" I screamed back. I heard the hot tub water pitching and sloshing over the edge and as my sight returned I saw the reason why. Two adults, one of them being my mother, and the other a man, had plopped their probably naked selves down in the water in a big, big hurry! My feet seemed glued to the deck and now I could see my mother covering her mouth, her eyes wide.

"Hey, Liz," the man in the hot tub said, smiling. "This is awkward, isn't it?" When I heard his voice, I realized the man was Mario DeLuca, a client of mine, and a big shot at the largest casino on the strip. Shaking with laughter, he took a sip of wine and said, "Why don't you wait for Susan in the kitchen, Liz, and I'll, uh, head out?" I saw his clothes, shoes and wallet on the umbrella table, so a quick exit actually seemed doable.

My twelve-year-old self surfaced briefly. *Gah, Mom in the hot tub with a guy who isn't Dad, gross!* Refusing to come any closer to them, I turned and headed toward the front door to let myself in and give them time to, uh, finish their business. Or whatever. The whole thing was even weirder because, though my parents hadn't lived together for years, my mom never actually divorced my dad.

When we met in the kitchen, we were both freaked out and tired, so we simply kissed each other good night. "Let's talk in the morning," Mom said.

The lines on Mom's face were noticeable in the morning light, but there was an unmistakable radiance there...the aura of a life well-lived? People say I look like her, and I can only hope to age as well as she has, despite six kids, and the many tough spots she's had to navigate. Part of it is, and always has been, because she doesn't take shit from anyone. Oh, well, she's taken plenty of shit from Dad, but she finally put a stop to that years ago.

"So…Mario, huh, Mom?"

She smiled. "I like him a lot, he's really fun. But then I hear you like Italian guys too, hmmm?"

How does she know? My mind went on search, search, search until I remembered Lilly's sister works in the same bank with my mom. *Damn, how MUCH does she know?* "So I guess you heard about Anthony?" I asked, disgusted with myself for the tentative sound of my voice. She went yakking on about it and various other tidbits of gossip from her work.

There was no trace of Lars awareness there, and I suddenly lost the nerve to tell her about it. She'd gotten so…Catholic lately, taking trips around her rosary beads every time she was worried about one of her six kids. Recently she put my first communion photo back up on the fireplace mantel. Yup, definitely lost my nerve. No frozen sperm revelation for Mother Susan, nope.

Mom was talking about the upcoming wedding of my brother Jack and his fiancée, Daniella. "This Thursday is her last night dancing with the show," my mom was saying. "She's starting to get big with their twins already!" Obviously gleeful about numbers two and three of her grandchildren, she added, "Let's all go see the show again! It'll be fun!" Daniella was one of the stars of *Romancing Vegas,* and it was no surprise she was having twins, since my brother Jack, her future husband, is a twin, and so are two of my other sisters, Anne and Ariana.

"Speaking of pregnancies, Mom, how old was Aunt Deb when she had Thomas?" My cousin Thomas was spoken of like the Immaculate Conception, born late to my mother's sister.

"She was forty-four years old, Liz. Why?" she asked, smiling coyly. "Changing your mind about having a child? Thinking about cooking up a Little Anthony with Anthony?"

I hit my forehead in mock humiliation. "Maa-uuum!" I sounded like a little kid, but my cheeks were pink, a telltale sign my mom picked up on. She grabbed her rosary.

"Mom, don't do patron saints, please!"

"Let's see, St. Gerard, patron saint of pregnancy, or how about St. Anthony? Maybe he's *your* patron saint of lost opportunities."

"Ha, ha, ha!" I fake-laughed and tried to change the subject. "You were only twenty when I was born, Mom. Do you ever regret it?"

"Oh no," she said emphatically. "Never! That first eighteen months with you, just you, were soooo wonderful. My perfect, beautiful little girl! And then when the twins were born, you were my best buddy." Her voice got a hitch in it and tears gathered in her eyes. "You were so sweet, helping me with all of them!" I put my arms around her, feeling the tears on her cheeks. She pulled back and looked me in the eye. "Have I ever thanked you Liz, truly thanked you for being there for me all those years?"

I patted her back. "I knew, Mom. I always knew you felt that way. It's okay." I guess it was my period, but soon I was crying, too. Wiping my tears, I asked "You seem to have gotten more religious lately, Mom. Any particular reason why?"

She smiled, wiping her tears. "They say as you get older, you realize you'd better start studying for the final exam."

Chuckling, I remembered to ask, "Oh, Mom, I'd like to get a ticket for Daniella's last show for Anthony, too. Can we do that?"

My mother winked. "Yeah, I know a guy from the Boca. You know him too!"

We went our separate ways to work. Mom told me weeks later the rosary she prayed that morning was asking God to say no to Lars and yes to Anthony. She *knew*. She knew the whole time and said nothing.

Chapter Twelve

A T HIS WIFE Serena's funeral, Anthony Anzione was painfully thin, the collar loose on his normally fastidious shirt. And you'd have to lose a lot of weight to make a bespoke Italian suit look as shapeless as Anthony's did that day. Even his trademark super-neat helmet of black hair had grown long, hanging over and under his collar.

He and his daughters held it together until the very end of the funeral, when it was time to walk away, leaving Serena there alone after her battle with breast cancer. That's when they let the tears flow, their sobs audible, clinging to each other as they staggered toward the limo.

More than two hundred mourners shuffled to their cars, and there wasn't a dry eye, mine included. We'd all known and liked Serena, and held up the Anziones as "the perfect couple," observing them at the many company events she attended when Anthony and I worked together at Lucidcom. There was plenty of work gossip about who was divorcing who, but Anthony and Serena seemed to prove a happy marriage could truly exist.

The day of Serena's funeral was the day I decided to start

my own company, Carleton Public Relations. On a day like that, it becomes crystal clear life is too short to trudge along in a corporate job you hate.

Still, thinking about Serena made me queasy. She was that woman you never wanted to be compared to, the very picture of a beautiful wife and mother who was also super-smart, gracious, and sexy. Parties at their house were always imaginative and fun, with her posse of girl and guy friends from all over town anointing the place with laughter. I just knew she would never have done some of the things I'd done, like let someone tie you up, or lust after someone else's husband. And she would certainly never, ever own a sex club!

And don't even get me started on the daughters, Lyndsey with her master's in social work, and Leah studying investment banking at Wharton. I mean what would she think about my plans for a chain of lifestyle clubs all over the country?!

But I decided to let it go for now.

Now it was four years after that funeral, and I was preparing for yet another kind of meeting with Anthony Anzione, but everything, and I mean *everything*, was different. A few weeks into our relationship, I was meeting his daughter, which must signify something. As good as it felt to think about it, I still resolved to keep my date with Lars next week. I'd gotten as far as meeting the family in my other relationships, but I couldn't trust it. I was still alone at forty.

"I'm a grown-up, people like me, and I'm not nervous." That was me giving myself a pep talk before meeting Anthony's daughter Leah for lunch at his favorite ravioli place. Did you ever imagine you'd still be doing that when you're forty? I was dressed in full-on corporate mode, wearing a skirted suit after a morning meeting, which I felt was unfortunate, because it might look like I was trying too hard.

Then when I walked into the restaurant, he introduced me to *both* his daughters *and* his sister Wendy! He shrugged and shook his head, as surprised as I was. Trying to soften the blow, he said, "Apparently Leah was talking to her aunt and her sister, and they all decided they need to get out of the office more. In Italian, they call this being a *ficcanaso*, a busybody." Wendy was enjoying Anthony's discomfort way too much, a smile quirking the corner of her mouth.

"It's okay, my family operates the same way," I said. "We'd all be trying to kick each other under the table right now." Still, this lunch with his family felt kind of like a job interview, one of those hellish moments when they say, "Tell us about yourself." Either that or a *60 Minutes* interview.

"Dad, did you get a different haircut?" Leah asked.

Anthony laughed. "Yeah, Liz told me I'd like it shorter because it gets so messed up when I'm working in the vineyard, sweating and wearing a hat all the time." The waitress came and took our orders for five different kinds of ravioli.

"Oh, so we've been saying it for years, and you don't change it, and she says one thing and you go get a haircut?" I looked at Leah, hoping she was joking and busting his chops about this, but she actually looked a little…pissed. Uh-oh.

Lyndsey chimed in. "Ick…the slicked-back sides on the old haircut—it had to go, Dad. Awful. This is much better."

"Yeah, didn't you once tell me it was too guido?" He grinned at his oldest child.

But all I could think about was how his soft lips and that sleek beard felt on my skin. Mmmm. *Okay, need to focus.*

Pointing to his haircut, Anthony asked the girls, "What do

you think about the way he tapered it into these shaved sides? It's very convenient this way, for wearing a hat and washing my hair, but is it too…gangsta?"

Lyndsey and Wendy thought this was hilarious. "Oh, ho, listen to you! Gangsta!?" they choked out. I enjoyed watching their interaction, which reminded me of hanging out with my family.

"Tell me, Liz, who are some of your clients?" Wendy asked, looking to bring the conversation around to me. It was the beginning of the "interview," but Wendy was throwing me the softball first.

"Believe it or not, we started out with Seasons Holdings. That was our first account!"

"Ohmigod, you were thinking *big*, Liz. Don't they own, like, six casinos?" It wasn't hard to guess that Wendy got people to talk for a living.

"Yeah, it was a total stroke of luck. I walked into their main office for laughs, to practice pitching my new company, and their management had decided *that week* they wanted to slim down their in-house staff and outsource PR. I know it helped when I agreed to hire three of their people, three fabulous people who knew the account like their own family, and who would otherwise have lost their jobs."

I laughed and glanced at Anthony, who had a smirk on his face. His raised eyebrows were signaling I was doing my nervous overtalking thing, but I'm sorry, I couldn't seem to help myself, so I kept going. "It was lucky, because they were my only employees at that point. We have ten people on the team now, and a diversified group of clients, along with Seasons, including a massive printing company, a restaurant group in Henderson, a construction company seeking government contracts, the dance show *Romancing Vegas*, and two luxury condos for people over fifty-five.

"Don't you also own La Vida, the, uh, swinger's club?" Leah asked, playing with her water glass.

Suddenly everyone at the table went completely still. Anthony's drink was suspended in midair, halfway to his mouth. The club's ownership was not public info, but I guess Leah dug it up somewhere on the internet.

Lyndsey leaned forward, eyes wide and said, "You own a...swinger's club?! Is it here in Las Vegas?"

Fortunately, I recovered quickly. "Yeah, I do. Totally by accident...isn't that crazy?! The owners were public relations clients, and they got in some financial trouble on other real estate they owned. I got a great deal on the property and the business. By the way, Leah, it's not a swinger's club. It's a private couple's social club. Couples come to the club for a night out with their spouse or partner."

"Right," Leah sneered, "a night out with their spouse and whatever other old perverts want to hook up with them. Aren't there rooms in the club where people have sex? Is that supposed to be normal?!" Lyndsey looked stunned, perhaps partly because her sister was being so flagrantly bitchy. Wendy was sitting back with her arms folded, taking it all in.

Anthony stood and pushed his chair back. "Leah, can you hear yourself right now? You are being deliberately rude, and I'd like you to come out to the lobby with me right now and explain yourself."

I put my hand on Anthony's arm to calm him. "It's okay, Anthony. I don't mind." I let a full minute go by, just sitting there and looking at Leah, thinking about the first time I'd ever heard about a club like La Vida, and putting myself in her shoes.

The food arrived, and everyone attacked their ravioli except for me and Leah. "Leah, you're starting out in life. Do you have a boyfriend?" She nodded, arms crossed over her chest. "Can you imagine for a minute what it would be like if, twenty years from now, you were doing the exact same things with him you're doing right now, whatever that might be?"

She shrugged, probably understanding my point but not wanting to. "I can't imagine that far into the future, but I could never imagine wanting to get my freak on at a sleazy place like that."

Anthony leaned forward, ready to jump in again, but I went first. "I respect that, Leah, but let's at least agree that owning La Vida is not who I am or what I'm about. It's simply something I happen to own that, believe it or not, people really enjoy. Can you accept that it might be true?"

"Sure," Leah answered, obviously unconvinced. She picked up her fork and didn't say another word or look at me until we all stood to leave, when she said "Nice meeting you," the smile on her face not reaching her eyes. Awkward? Meeting Leah had turned out to be the *definition* of awkward!

Lyndsey was right behind her, but gave me a little hug first, and said, "I'm sorry, not sure what that was about."

Wendy walked next to me and patted my shoulder as we trailed behind the girls. "That went well, didn't it?" she said, and we laughed, breaking up the tension. "I do want to say in her defense that my brother hasn't introduced them to anyone since Serena died. I'll talk to her...give it a couple days first, and then see where her head's at."

Looking over at her brother, she added, "Anthony, my advice to you is to let her talk to you if she wants to, and then remember God gave you two ears and one mouth, so listen twice as much as you talk. Capiche?" He rolled his eyes at her and they hugged. Their rapport made me miss my brothers Cole and Jack, and I resolved to call them tonight, no matter where in the world they might be.

As we all finally spilled out onto the sidewalk, ready to

head our separate ways, we heard the shriek of a police siren and the loud chatter of official radio, the strobe lights on top of the cruisers bouncing off the surrounding buildings. Four or five policemen were searching a car in the parking lot, the doors and the trunk open. And the car in the center of all that activity was my car.

Chapter Thirteen

Anthony

COULD IT GET any worse? On the day Liz met my family, one of my daughters decided to pick a fight with her about owning a sex club, and the police found drugs in Liz's car within plain sight of my sister and daughters.

They all had to get back to work, and Wendy squeezed my hand in sympathy, but it was hard not to see the doubt in their eyes about *who* this woman I was seeing could possibly be. I phoned the office and had them cancel the rest of my appointments while Liz and I talked to the police. Luckily, the lead detective was Manuel Ortiz, a guy I'd done some work for. "How do you know him?" Liz asked as we headed over to the police station in my car. Her car was now evidence.

"I represented his family in an estate situation when his father died."

Liz was agitated, and rightly so, fidgeting in her seat and texting her office. "Are you, uh, coming along as my friend or my attorney, Anthony? You don't do this type of criminal stuff usually, do you? I have a criminal lawyer, Josh Levine,

who handled a stalking thing involving my sister last year."
Her question was an excellent one, and I was glad to see she
was still thinking on her feet in spite of being understandably
agitated.

"Levine has a great reputation. Why don't you see if he
can meet us at the station? I'm here as your friend, and as
your friend, I'd advise you not to talk to the police until he
joins us. And because I'm not your attorney, I can say that
I'm pretty sure this drug thing has to do with *your* stalkers in
your office park, the Morrows. Did you know the civil suit
they filed against you was dropped yesterday, dismissed due
to lack of evidence?"

Liz had tears in her eyes and touched my hand, her voice
tinged with sarcasm. "You mean the one asking for damages
because of the—she lifted her free hand to do air quotes—
emotional distress and mental anguish I've caused? No, I did
not know it was settled yet, but thank you, and thanks for
keeping your ear to the ground."

She covered her eyes, and her shoulders shook with sobs
as the adrenaline drained out of her, probably leaving a
tangle of fear and disbelief brewing in her gut. "Oh, my God,
Anthony, the first day when she threatened me, she had this
weird smile on her face that never changed. When she was
doing the petition mess, she pointed a finger at me and said,
'We're going to get you, make no mistake about that.' I
guess this is it, she's finally got me. First, the restraining
order, then the civil suit, and now this. They just won't
quit!" Reaching out to me again, she whispered, "I'm so
sorry you had to get dragged into this. And, worse yet, in
front of your family."

We walked through a stereotypical precinct office lined
with grey metal desks, and overheard someone saying "La
Vida? Oh, yeah. They probably do a lot of drugs in a place

like that." Liz stopped and stood stock still, looking around for the source of the comment, her jaw set and fists clenched. Luckily, the ignorant asshole who said those words was nowhere in our sight, because Liz looked ready to ream the guy a new one. Personally, I was glad we overheard it, because it revealed a negative mindset that would never have occurred to me.

Ortiz was very courteous and went strictly by the book, waiting for Josh Levine, and then filling us in on exactly what they found in Liz's car—a bag of marijuana and two bags of prescription painkillers labeled MYDOSE Pill Pouch—as well as describing the anonymous phone call leading to the search of her car.

I hate to admit it, but even I watched Liz's face very carefully when the detective described the drugs and the phone call, saw her mouth fly open, eyes wide, and hands gripping the arms of the chair so tightly her knuckles were white.

He asked her the obvious questions about prescription drug use, and Liz didn't even seem to know what Vicodin and Percocet were for, much less be looking forward to her next pain fix. They had to conclude either she knew absolutely nothing about it, or she was an Oscar-worthy actress. In a calm, even voice, Liz stated that she believed the drugs were planted in her car by the Morrows because of a mistaken belief they had about an incident of spray-painting vandalism.

His hands folded on the table, Ortiz said, "Tell us your story from the beginning, Ms. Carleton, starting with when and how you know the Morrows, and when and how the spray-painting incident occurred."

She blushed a little when she began, knowing Ortiz and Levine were assessing her as the owner of a club where mysterious, naughty things happened. When she described it as a private social club for couples, they seemed confused, as it didn't match their own ideas about what La Vida was. As an attorney, I was allowed in the room, and I nodded at her, hoping to remind her we talked about giving only the facts, not too many details.

"They used to be great neighbors, the Morrows. They kept to themselves, generally coming in the early evening before my club opens. They had a complaint about cigarette butts once, they're super-neat...but anyway, it is a parking lot. They have this painting on the side of their truck, a picture of a quaint little antique shop like one in a movie, the same as the image on their website. Their actual place here is just a warehouse, though. The shop is only online.

"So I saw the spray paint all over the image on the truck on a Friday about 7 pm, about two hours before we open. It was black and red paint with words like 'loser' and 'fuck' on there, too. They were standing there by the truck, waiting for the police, and I stopped by to say I was sorry it happened to them. They asked me a few questions, like was I open last night, and did I see anything, and they seemed to be getting angrier as we talked.

"They must have decided I was gloating and had gone over to comfort them about the damage, and they took it as an admission I knew the spray painting was done by one of my customers, or that I did it myself. When the policeman got there, Jane Morrows asked me 'How can you live with yourself, defacing someone's property like that? I don't know how you can sleep at night.' I mean, totally crazy, right? And no matter what I said, she always kept the same weird smile on her face."

When talking about Jane Morrows, Liz seemed genuinely frightened. After Ortiz stood up to leave, she told him what she told me. "Oh, I forgot. Jane Morrows pointed her finger at me after no one would sign her petition to get rid of me and my business, and she said 'We will get you.'" Sighing, she leaned back in her chair. "I guess this is what she meant."

Ortiz gathered his papers, looking at me and Levine. "As you know, Ms. Carleton has no record, not even a traffic ticket, and because she has family and two businesses in Las Vegas, we don't believe she's a flight risk. Don't make me regret that I'm releasing her without bail on her own recognizance, okay Anzione?"

Levine waited until we hit the sidewalk before he huddled us up and said "Liz, I don't have to tell you this is serious. They dug up the info about the club, and that's a bit of a shadow on your perfect profile. They might try to cut corners and treat this as a slam dunk, not doing all the investigation and testing they should do. They had probable cause because the anonymous phone caller described you as driving the car erratically and the driver appearing high, and that's all they needed to justify checking it out."

"What about the caller? Didn't the dispatcher have caller ID?" I asked.

"Yeah. Unfortunately, the call was made from a business center at the Gold Rush Hotel. Anybody can use that phone."

"Honestly, Josh," Liz said, "isn't it obvious the phone caller knew exactly what to say to create a probable cause situation? Like *two lawyers*, for instance?!"

"Good point Liz, but still...we have to..."

I interrupted. "What about running DNA on the drugs?"

"I asked Ortiz about it. It costs thousands of dollars, and we have to build a case for the judge before they'd allow it for a little bust like this."

A bust that could totally ruin Liz's reputation, but I didn't say that out loud. We probably made quite a sight, three suits standing there on the sidewalk lost in thought.

Josh Levine looked Liz directly in the eye. "Liz, if you submit to a cheek swab and a search of your apartment, right now before you go home, how will it turn out?"

I took her hand. "He's asking you without asking you if drugs will show up in your system or your apartment."

"Absolutely not," Liz said with no hesitation. "Let's do it."

"How about a polygraph, a lie-detector test? Would it influence the judge to test DNA on the drugs?" I asked.

"That would help, too," Levine said. "Would you be willing to pay for it yourself? It would cost a couple hundred bucks. It also would help expedite the process, and we could do it tomorrow. I want to be here for it, so text me the appointment time as soon as you have it," he said as he hurried away down the sidewalk.

Liz couldn't walk back into the station fast enough for her cheek swab, and you could see the policemen who took the swab, and the one who ran through the paperwork with her on the apartment search, grudgingly admiring her moxie. They see so many scared victims that it must be refreshing for them to see someone who's got it together enough to jump through these hoops and *make* innocence happen. I know I was proud to be standing at her side.

I walked Liz to her office building, holding her hand and apologizing for my daughter's snottiness at lunch about ten times in ten different ways. "Maybe you should come to *my* office," I said, kissing her hand. "You stated your case so well, I think maybe we should trade places for the day."

"Uh, no thanks," she said, "but the ravioli was great."

My voice was a little tentative when I asked, "See you tonight?"

"Absolutely!" she answered, and planted a huge, cheerful

kiss on my cheek. "Oh, by the way, do you want to see *Romancing Vegas* on Thursday night? It's my future sister-in-law's last show, so, fair warning, family members, including my mom, will be there."

I gave her a little salute. "I'm up for the job, Liz. Can't wait!"

Chapter Fourteen

Liz

"ANTHONY ANZIONE, I am so pissed off by your effortless hotness, even while wearing a pink shirt. Speaking of pink, what is this?" I raised my glass, admiring the bright fruit and the little striped umbrella.

He'd noticed I tend to order pink drinks, so now he made a game of it, ordering a different one every time we went out. As usual, all the females in the bar were watching Anthony's every sexy move, his perpetual tan highlighted by the shirt and his super-white smile.

"It's called Sex on the Beach. Rum, a little peach schnapps, a little cranberry juice. You and I need to find a beach at some point, don't you think?" Anthony had a way of looking into my eyes that made me burn from the inside out. "And let me remind you the pink shirt was your idea, by the way." Anthony's trademark white shirts were great, of course. He only bought this one when I teased him that his entire closet was either black or white.

He showed up for my lie detector test yesterday, even though my lawyer had it covered. I was feeling optimistic again after giving my cheek swab, doing the polygraph, and presiding over the search of my apartment. No drugs in my system *or* my apartment! How about THAT, Your Honor?!

Everything went well, and we were actually a little surprised we hadn't heard from Josh Levine that morning saying the DNA test had been authorized. We dotted all the i's and crossed the t's. What could be holding us up? Though he was trying not to let on, I could tell Anthony was worried.

I hesitated last night before I took the Clomid pill that would increase my chances of getting pregnant next week, thinking about the dynamics at lunch with Anthony's family. I knew from bitter experience how those things could pop the little bubble Anthony and I were living in right now. So I forced myself to picture the tiny baby who had become my heart's desire, and swallowed that sucker with a full glass of water. My restless dreams alternated between visions of a baby wearing a Viking hat and making love with Anthony while eating ravioli.

Snapping back into the here and now, I sipped my drink. It was delicious, but soooo strong! "Okay, so here's my short summary on pink drinks. Everyone wants women to get tipsy, especially bartenders, because it's entertaining, and people buy more drinks. So that's why you get more alcohol in a pink drink. Just sayin', you get *such* a deal!"

We were in the Boca Casino, at the bar right outside the entrance to *Romancing Vegas*. It got noticeably louder when my family walked in, Mom, my sister Sara, and my twin sisters Anne and Ariana.

Anthony got with the hug program right away, ignoring my mom's outstretched hand to go in immediately for the polite embrace. Good instincts. The Carleton family would be suspicious of anyone who didn't hug.

"I'm so glad you could come," I squeezed Sara. "Who'd you get to watch Abigail?" Sara's husband is deployed in

Afghanistan, and she and her daughter were living with our mom.

Speaking softly in my ear, she said "You're not gonna believe this, but Dad is staying with her. He's been coming around once a week since you guys had that big meeting with him."

My brothers, my mom, and I talked out some issues with my dad a couple of months ago, but I was surprised Mom trusted him enough, even now, to leave him with full responsibility for her only grandchild. She didn't want him to talk with any of us for years, but suddenly grandpa duty? And then there's the pesky little side issue that Mom is still married to Dad and dating Mario. WTF?!

Mom, Ariana, and Anne seemed to be having a lively conversation with Anthony, and I arrived just in time to see Mom pick up my drink and say, "This drink is so pretty! I want to order one. What is it called?" Anthony's eyebrows were *all* the way up!

Grabbing it and sipping nonchalantly, I said, "It's called Sex on the Beach, Mom. Want me to order one for you?"

My sisters thought this was hilarious of course, but Mom surprised all of us. She turned to the bartender and said, "Could I have four Sex on the Beaches, please? Or would that be Sexes on the Beach? Whatever. We'd like four, please."

The young bartender dude was trying so hard not to laugh, but his dimples gave him away. "I'll need to see ID from everyone, including you ma'am." It was pretty comical to see my Mom dig through her gigantic purse for her wallet, but it gave Anthony the opportunity to jump in and pay the tab for the drinks.

There was a flurry of phone selfies and group photos of the Carleton ladies holding the pink drinks, and soon it was time to go into the theater. Of course, Mario got us great seats to watch Daniella Flores—soon to be Daniella Carleton—rock the house in one of the opening numbers, "The History of Booty." Starting with Meghan Trainor's "All About That Bass," and pulsing through five costume changes and six decades of booty-shaking songs, Daniella led the dancers through a breathtaking routine without even seeming to break a sweat.

I couldn't tell Daniella was pregnant because I'd only seen the show once before, and she looked voluptuous and amazing to me, but my mother was all, like, "Awww, look at her belly," waving and blowing her kisses. Like most Vegas shows, *Romancing Vegas* moved at a blistering pace through all ninety minutes of production numbers that included sexy aerialists, a knife-throwing dominatrix, and a world-renowned juggler named Sergei.

Oksana Shevchenko, the show's star and producer, came out at the end of the show and brought Daniella up for a special final curtain call, handing her an armful of red roses. "Daniella Flores was not only the first dancer to jump into this crazy show with me, she was also very important in every single step of its creation! Now she is embarking on a new production, the creation of, not one, but two little people who are destined to make this world a better place." They cried and hugged each other while the crowd jumped to its feet, applauding not only Daniella's artistry, but the obvious sisterhood between the two women.

We hung out with Daniella after the show until she confessed to being really, really bone tired and kissed us all goodnight. Mario came to scoop up my mom and take her somewhere for a late bite. "You know Mario?" Anthony asked.

"He's a client, and he got us these tickets."

"Hey, he's a client of mine, too. I'm going to grab him and

talk privately for a sec." We shook hands with Mario, and Anthony was real smooth, asking Mom if he could borrow Mario for a minute. My mom didn't seem to think twice, and I figured they were talking about me and my case, but neither one of them looked over. Super-smooth, like I said.

After that, Anthony and I were swept along into the Boca's nightclub with my sisters and some young performers from the show. We hung outside for a minute, and Anthony said quietly, "I figured Mario might know a guy who knows the judge, ya' know? And he actually does."

"Aaaayyy," I said. "Now *he's* connected!" and we both laughed.

While drinking way too much premium booze because of the bottle service arranged for us by Mario, my sisters and I entertained Anthony with tales of growing up in a big family. He enjoyed the stories about our loud arguments and louder holidays, and the funny work-arounds we had to do to afford basic things. My sisters loved Anthony's mad dancing skills, out on the dance floor holding his own with the dancers from the show, and it was an all 'round great evening.

"You're so excited about Daniella's twins," Anthony said to me as we settled into a cab back to my place. "Did you ever think about having a kid?"

And there it was, alive and kicking, the elephant was IN the room...er, the cab. What I should have said was "You know, I've actually been meaning to tell you about something very important," but instead I said, "What? And have another person running around the house who is crazier than I am?" I didn't want to ruin a great evening, we were both drunk, and it wasn't a good time. I had a legion of excuses to pick from for why I didn't tell Anthony the truth right then.

"But your family, they make it look fun," Anthony said as he guided my drowsy feet into the apartment. "I mean, Wendy and I had each other, but you guys had an army, a freaking tribe!" It was almost like he was living the big family vicariously.

"You're just lucky my brothers weren't there tonight. They're even better drinkers than those Ukrainian dancers we were with! Or do I mean worse?" I sighed and lay my head on his shoulder. "I'm glad you like my family."

That's the last thing I remember until I woke up the next morning, hungover and alone. Since it was Friday, it wasn't surprising Anthony had to rush into the office, but it was strange he didn't leave a note or send a text.

Chapter Fifteen

Anthony

FOR ME, A hangover headache is different from an allergy headache. When it's allergies, the pain is right between my eyes. With alcohol, the diffuse headache comes with all-over lousy; there's a reason "intoxicated" has the word "toxic" in it. Liz was fast asleep when I began plundering her medicine cabinet for a hangover cure. I saw the ibuprofen hiding in the back and grabbed it, knocking a prescription bottle into the sink.

When I picked it up, these words jumped out: *Clomid Take one pill each day on days 5 through 9 of cycle.* I remembered Serena taking this when we were having difficulty conceiving Leah. It causes women to ovulate, or to make more eggs, or…anyway, it makes it easier to get pregnant. The refill was dated last week, but my mouth went completely dry when I read the name of the patient—Elizabeth Carleton.

Okay, this probably isn't a big deal. There must be some other purpose for taking this drug, or else why would Liz be taking a fertility drug? I let out a shaky breath, searching through my brain for the pieces of each other we'd shared, intimate pieces that didn't include any mention of a fertility drug. Our relationship felt too new—and too important—to simply blurt out the question.

My hangover headache was killing me, but right at that moment, I couldn't wait to get out of there and get home. *Was I being naïve? Was she only playing the part of my perfect lover, and actually had a completely different goal in mind?*

Liz had plans with her mom that weekend, which was suddenly and urgently okay with me. I walked quietly out of the bedroom, glancing at Liz sleeping peacefully, her hair spread out on the pillow. When I got to the car, I checked out Clomid on my phone and then shut it down, driving home in a detached, energetic fury. They say one of the best ways to recover from a hangover was a little hair o' the dog, and I was about to find out.

"Anthony, you okay? What's going on? Lyndsey called me because you haven't been answering the phone, and she's worried. Why are you here in the dark in your underwear?" My sister had her customary top o' the mornin' mood going, all smiles, sunshine, and peppy walk.

I was finding it hard to open my mouth. It was glued shut from drinking, sleeping, not talking, and not brushing my teeth for two days. "How did you get in?" I managed to choke out, blinking at her knees from my belly-down position on the couch. Lifting my head to make eye contact seemed far too painful.

"Lyndsey told me where you keep the key."

Taking in the empty bottles of wine and pizza boxes lying around, she yelled over my third viewing of *Silver Linings Playbook* "What kind of a shit show is this? It stinks in here."

Turning off the TV and sitting cross-legged on the floor, she was now firmly in my face. "Whatever this is, it's stupid," she said, studying me frankly. "I feel certain it has something to do with Liz, because she's the only one who's gotten Stone Cold Anthony out of the freezer lately."

It was amazing to me that plugging away at my job and keeping my life neat and tightly controlled was considered by the three women in my life as being in the freezer. Careening around Vegas with a woman who was lying to me, or at least not telling me the whole truth, was apparently synonymous with being warm and alive.

Pushing a lock of greasy hair out of my face, she asked "So what's up?"

"Nothing is up. Everything is down. Can't you see that?" My voice sounded hung over, even to me, partially because I was speaking into the couch cushions. "I read a study that being excessively happy causes you to engage in riskier behaviors, so now I'm good."

After ripping a pillow out from under my forehead, Wendy put it under her head as she lay flat on the floor. Now her voice was a disembodied thing rising from the floor. "By risky behaviors, I guess you mean having sex with, and opening yourself up to, another person."

I turned over and talked to the ceiling too. "Yes, those behaviors have proven risky."

Tick, tock, tick, tock. Wendy's silence stretched out into the infinite range as she waited me out. I surrendered. "Liz, uh...I found fertility drugs in her bathroom. The prescription was filled last week, with Liz's name on it. Serena took it; it helps women release more eggs. There's no other use for that drug."

There were a few too many beats of silence. She cleared her throat, literally "ahem," and said, in a flat voice, "Gotta say, didn't see that one coming."

"I'm lying here wondering...does Liz see me as a sperm bank, a cash machine, or both?"

I reached my hand down to Wendy, and she took it, and kept calmly listening.

"This just seems so…unlike the vibe I've been getting from Liz, a good vibe, like we could go somewhere. I've puzzled out her situation for two days. Yeah, cliché, she turned forty and might want a kid. But she seems to be financially stable—no, better than stable. Why tap me for…whatever?"

"Do you guys use condoms?"

"We do. But she said she would soon be able to go without, my take being she'd gone on the pill. But not *this* pill, you know? I guess if she was pregnant, we wouldn't have to use condoms. Is that where this is going, me getting trapped into eighteen years of supporting a kid?"

I took a deep breath and paused, squeezing her hand. "God. I am so confused. Remember when we couldn't wait to grow up and make our own decisions, our own painful, life-changing decisions? What were we thinking, Wendy? Being a kid was great!"

Wendy got up and sat in the chair across from me, apparently galvanized by an idea. "Childhood was great, but what about raising kids, wasn't that great?"

I started to say something, but she held up her hand. "Bear with me a minute." Her words tumbled over each other like kittens in a basket. "If you were going into this together, would you want to do it if she asked? Or is the idea too awful? Have you said things that would tell her you're glad child-raising is over? Also, what's the worst part of this nondisclosure for you? Is it the idea of raising a kid, or the idea of her deceiving you?"

I answered without hesitation. "The deception. That's the worst." The despair I felt since I found those pills was a reality check, showing me how addicted to Liz I'd become.

"So you don't totally hate the idea of having a kid with her?"

"Uhh…I'm not sure. I have to think about that one. I may have dropped some 'I'm glad that's over' remarks."

"Is there someone close to her you could talk to and find out if there's something else, something you don't know, that's going on?"

"There's Lilly, her best friend. She's a casino host at the Flynn. I could probably get in touch with her."

Wendy grabbed her purse and keys. "I have a patient, have to go. You have two ways to go. Drop it like it's hot, or call her friend and puzzle this out. It's up to you, bro."

I chuckled at her Snoop Dogg reference, feeling myself peeking out from the grave, if not actually rising from the dead yet. "Well, thanks a lot, House-Call Shrink."

"All good. Let me know how it turns out. One thing is, you never learned how to relax and spend money on yourself like normal people anyway. What're you gonna do for the next ten years, take up golf?"

Wendy and I both knew how ridiculous *that* was. Neither of us felt like a worthy human being unless we were creating *something*. "A kid would be a great new project for you, especially since your previous results are excellent. The kind of chemistry you two have, the peculiar history…it's rare. I'd call Lilly, if it was me."

My sister, when she has her shrink hat on, rarely makes that kind of prejudicial statement. So I called Lilly.

You could hear Lilly's wheels turning when I called. "Uh…haaeey, Anthony, how are ya'?"

"Good Lilly. I… I'd like to have a private conversation with you, one you don't share with Liz for right now. What do you think?"

Both Lilly and Liz are quick thinkers, and she answered immediately. "I think...it would depend on what's good for Liz. If it's not good for Liz, I wouldn't want to talk with you about anything. So...pardon my casino parlance, but it's a crap shoot for you Anthony. If you ask me about something that sucks for her, she'll be my next call, got it?"

"Everyone needs a friend like you, Lilly!" I cringed but laughed at her honesty. *Oh, what the hell.* "Okay, here's my shot. When I was looking for ibuprofen in Liz's medicine cabinet, I found a newly-filled prescription of Clomid with Liz's name on it. You know what that is, and you can imagine what I'm wondering, right?"

There was a period of silence on the other end of the line and then Lilly started stumbling around. "Wait...how...I mean, you must've...uh, oh shit!" My stomach sank. Maybe this was as bad as I feared. Sperm donor/cash machine bad. "So what exactly do *you* think it means, Anthony?"

I try to answer questions like that with a question, just like she did. "I guess what I'm asking is, does she want to use my sperm to have a kid without asking me first?"

"Does she want to...without...ohmigod! Is *that* what you think?!" Lilly started laughing on the other end of the line, a big relieved-sounding laugh with a heeya, heeya to it. This went on for some minutes before she settled down to a breathless chuckle and picked up the phone she'd dropped.

"Okay, it was funny at first," she was still laughing, kind of a hee hee hee now, "but now I get where you're coming from. You're a lawyer, so you're thinking paternity and child support etcetera. However, because I think you two are good together, I'll tell you what's going on...if YOU promise not to tell Liz I told you." Quiet for a minute, she chuckled again and added, "Do I sound like we're in fifth grade, passing notes?"

"I don't think kids pass notes anymore, Lilly. They text each other now. Anyway, yeah, tell me what's going on, because this situation seems so unlike Liz." Notice in that sentence it *sounded* like I agreed not to tell, but I *didn't* agree, because I would tell if it made sense to do so. Sorry, plausible deniability. I'm a lawyer, after all.

Anyway, Lilly told me the story of Liz and her sperm donor nicknamed Lars, the many reasons she was going the sperm-in-a-jar route, and the fact that Liz's first insemination failed, and the second one was supposed to be next Wednesday. She told me, "These things are timed to ovulation you know, and, strictly speaking, the sperm don't come in a jar, they come frozen in a cryovac container. Then you test for pregnancy in 16 days."

Lilly offered to tell me some sperm jokes, but I passed on it and thanked her, asking "You know Liz's calendar. Do you think she can get away, like for four days?" I'd had a crazy revelation while Lilly and I were talking.

"I don't know of anything special going on. I'll keep my mouth shut if you make something good happen. Why don't you ask her?"

Chapter Sixteen

Liz

"**I**S THIS THING…yours?!" I was in awe of the noisy, shiny helicopter, his familiarity with the digital doodads, and his sexy voice checking with the tower.

"No, I'm in kind of a timeshare where we each reserve a certain number of uses. I go out about ten times a year." When he reached over and tightened the straps on my seat's harness, he flashed me a smile. "You look good in this!" Obviously he was remembering my rope bra from the club, and we both laughed.

I babbled, "Oh dear god, there's a scene in *Fifty Shades of Grey* like this, where he straps her in tight! Do you feel like a millionaire playboy?! Where did you learn to fly a helicopter?" He shook his head and gave me a peck on the cheek, laughing at my adolescent excitement. "And are you sure you're well enough to fly this thing? You said you were so sick you couldn't even answer my texts!"

"I'm healed, feeling good. As far as flying, I went to college on an Air Force ROTC scholarship. During my service, I flew an Apache helicopter in the invasion of Panama, the one they called Operation Just Cause." Lips pressed tight, he added, "We found out later it was *not* a just cause, but we didn't know. When I found out the so-called bad guy we were chasing was on the CIA payroll, I didn't reenlist, and became a lawyer instead."

Immediately I flashed to Serena being the perfect Air Force wife, creating a home for them wherever they were stationed. Once again, I couldn't help beating myself up that my track record was woefully inadequate in the long-term relationship department.

The hours flew by, because, let's face it, traveling in a helicopter is like being Peter Pan or Superman. You can see stuff, but get from one place to another in no time, bypassing all the traffic, aggravating drivers, and gritty dumpsters by the side of the road. Everything looks pretty and clean from the air, even the smog-draped skyscrapers and the snarl of cars crawling bumper to bumper on California's highways.

"So I guess Mario *did* know a guy who knew the judge, eh?" I reached into my purse and pulled out my tablet, finding the article about police arresting the Morrows for harassing me.

"I love how the headline on the article read 'Don't like your neighbor? Plant drugs in their car!'" Anthony laughed.

I gave him a dramatic reading of the details of how the drugs they planted in my car had the Morrows' DNA all over it, and none of mine. And when they opened up the Morrows' medicine cabinet, their medications were kept in MYDOSE Pill Pouches, exactly like the ones in my so-called stash! And how the security footage from the hotel where the anonymous call was made showed Keith Morrows entering the business center minutes before the call was made.

Ortiz was laughing, out-of-control *laughing* when he called my lawyer. He said Jane Morrows was wearing a negligee when they picked her up, expecting her secret boyfriend to be at the door. She was pretty surprised when it was the police, reading her rights before they arrested her. The husband was at a tennis lesson when they cuffed him.

"All the articles had the same point of view," Anthony said, "They portrayed the Morrows as a mean-spirited power couple, and you as a hard-working business owner; the story had kind of a David and Goliath vibe."

I ducked my head. "Yeah that's me, the brave pipsqueak fighting the slick lawyers who screwed up royally. My office *might* have written a rough draft of the article and passed it on to some reporters. Of course, the reporters verified everything, but they loved the crazy, vengeful lawyers angle. People love it when rich folks think they're too smart to fail."

Anthony shot me the side eye, chuckling and shaking his head.

"Hey, I have a public relations firm. I needed to handle my own PR, didn't I?!" I grabbed his hand over the console. "Seriously though, I do appreciate you being there for me through every aspect of this mess." He squeezed my hand, picked it up, and kissed it.

My stomach was a little grumbly, and I felt tired and sleepy from the Clomid, but I fought the urge to close my eyes. Anthony was vibrating with excitement, obviously enjoying being at the helm of this expensive, complicated machine. "Have you driven in California?" he asked as I wrinkled my nose at the chaotic highways below, the ones paralleling the Pacific Coast Highway.

"I have. It's interesting. I was almost assaulted once by a self-righteous bicyclist riding in the car lane. He said I was following too close! It seemed so…California."

His voice was amplified by the headsets, his laugh seeming

even deeper than usual. "And yet native Californians seem to feel stop signs and red lights are optional. You know what Neil Simon said about California?"

"Neil Simon, the playwright?"

"Yeah. When he first moved here from New York, he said the problem with California is that it's just one goddamn nice day after another!" We laughed, the quote striking both of us as exactly what a smart, crabby New Yorker would say. There're so many NYC transplants in Las Vegas and LA (including Anthony), these days they're considered New York West.

He fumbled around on some kind of radio, and the Disney song *A Whole New World* came on. Now we were choking with laughter, the similarity of Aladdin's magic carpet to our magical helicopter silly but incredibly amusing. *This is what it's like to get to know someone, to take the time to draw them out, hear what's on their mind, and create some shared experiences.* It had been so long since I had a relationship with a man who wasn't playing mind games with me that I'd forgotten how…easy it is. Easy to enjoy, hard to find.

Looking over at my pilot, I was filled with yearning, with the desire to know and love the man, *this* man, who could make the little blue line appear on a pregnancy test. Who doesn't want that?

When I finally accepted that my ability to have children the traditional way was on too long a time line, I looked at the bright side—I got to shop for the perfect father! Still, it was hitting me at that moment that Lars the Sperm Donor might be a physicist who sidelines as a male model, but does he have a sense of humor? Is that even genetic, or should I leave the Comedy Channel on 24/7 for a few years?

Anthony and I could talk about the least sexy things in the world, but I was still drawn to him, drawn to the strength in those hands of his, one minute gripping the throttle, the other letting it slide through his fingers. He had a way of doing that with me too, one minute making me feel grounded and safe, the next pushing and challenging me to do new things.

I had a strong feeling I could share my dreams with him and he wouldn't judge me, but it was so damned early in our relationship. Those warm eyes of his drew me in, made me want to believe we could be partners, making this baby together, raising it together.

Then my mind replayed his voice saying *I finally have money and time to spend on myself.*

I had to make a decision at some point. Let him go *before* I got pregnant? Or get pregnant and horrify him in real time, wringing every thrill out of our relationship until he walked (or probably ran) in the opposite direction? But I didn't have to decide today. Not today.

Soon we approached the Los Padres National Forest, a sea of green trees with a mist floating silently above it. Playing tour guide, Anthony said, "The redwoods in northern California are the tallest trees in the world. Some of them live 2,000 years or more, and have root systems that extend 100 miles." We're both such nerds, I realized, getting an equal charge knowing and sharing stupid factoids like that! We liked museums and musical theater. I'd never been with anyone else who enjoyed that kind of thing.

When we cleared the forest and approached the coast, the sky seemed vast, endless, especially from this height. We landed on a helipad behind a very pleasant-looking resort, and I hoped people saw us as we climbed out of our sleek celebrity ride.

Our room was beautiful, and the first thing I did was walk

out to our private balcony and let the fresh air fill my lungs while I took in the breathtaking view of Big Sur—the cliffs, beaches, and crashing surf.

He was right behind me when I cried, "Anthony, look! It's a condor!" His arms tight around me, we watched the bird soar, its ten-foot wingspan starkly black against the blue sky. "It's so huge, it…looks like a glider or an airplane!" The bird seemed to fly directly into a cliff, probably into its nest, and disappeared.

Anthony's hands covered mine, resting on the railing as we both took in some of the most majestic scenery in the world. Our relationship up to this point was like being on a series of fun daytrips away from the grind of our careers, but being in this place was like living in a bubble, for sure. I loved how wonderful it felt to be away—*with him*—from our everyday lives. Still, there was an achy spot in my chest when I pondered the probable end of our sexy holidays.

The warmth of his body behind me filled me with the same conflicting emotions as always, comfort and need. I turned toward him and asked, "Is there something special about this place for you? Did you come here with…" my voice trailed off, not wanting to break the spell we were both feeling. "Do you have a special connection with this place?"

"I actually heard about it from a client. It's luxurious, but there are no televisions, alarm clocks or phones in these suites. I'm putting my cell on vibrate." Hands cupping my face, he said "I want to know you, Liz. I have equally big plans for learning about you and making you come. I'm taking a crash course in Liz this weekend."

The way he said it, the intense look in his eyes, thrilled me. Part of me wanted to turn away, afraid I might be burned by his honesty, but most of me wanted to witness it, to receive his words in all their raw passion.

"I don't know, Anthony," I drawled, trying to keep a teasing tone in my voice. "You often seem to know what's happening with me even before *I* know what's happening with me." It was spooky how often he seemed to figure me out and offer me something I didn't know I wanted. Coming here with him, for example. The timing was completely weird, and yet completely right at the same time, allowing us to drink our fill of each other before my next shot at conceiving a baby.

"Liz. I need to…" He ran his fingers along my jaw, light as the condor's flight, but just as powerful. Pointing to a long stretch of beach to our right, he said, "Let's go for a walk."

Carrying a bag to put our sandals in, we stopped at the concierge and made a reservation for dinner in the hotel's famous restaurant. Pointing at the bag, the concierge said "Mind the tide down there, but there's no need to carry a bag. There are cubbies on the beach to leave your sandals, and no one will bother them." She winked. "We want to facilitate maximum holding of hands while walking the beach."

And hold hands we did, walking in silence on the sand, sea foam bubbling and popping around our ankles. I couldn't remember the last time I'd been to the beach, and I'd forgotten how soothing, how spirit-expanding it could be. Picking up some interesting pebbles and pointing out some unusual colors low on the horizon, I was doing all the talking. Anthony Anzione acted like he had something to say, something he found difficult to talk about.

Scooping up a handful of foam, he held it out for closer examination. "You know how you make whipped cream, essentially by whipping air into it? That's what the ocean waves do, pumping air into water and making this foam. It's basically a bunch of air bubbles stuck together."

I played along with his nerdy procrastination. "And what

are the bubble colors from, the purple, green and yellow iridescence?"

"*That* is electrodynamics," he said, wiggling his eyebrows at me. "But I guess you know I don't really want to talk about particle physics, right?"

I nodded, grinning.

"I…when you almost asked if I came here with Serena, when you ask about things we did together, I see you're constantly comparing yourself with her. You have to stop. What you and I have…it's different. I guess I need to tell you some things about it, about her. A few things that are true but not exactly…positive."

I stopped, facing him, and keeping myself as still as possible, wanting him to know *I* knew how important this was, but not wanting to judge in *any* way.

"Serena and I were high school sweethearts, and then we went to college at Adelphi together since we were both living at home and commuting to college. Serena was on the pill, but took antibiotics for an infection and…nine months later Lyndsey was born. She never finished college, and we were nineteen when we married, three months before the baby was born. We traveled around the country while I was in the Air Force, and I was recruited by Lucid while I was in law school here in Vegas. When you met me, when you saw us at that club, it was right before her diagnosis." I touched the side of his face, brushing a tear away.

His mouth was trembling as he struggled with his feelings, but he pulled me in for a hug before he continued. "I guess the story I'm trying to tell here is that we were so young. Between raising the girls, and then dealing with breast cancer, Serena wasn't very…sexual. She went to Catholic school, and she struggled with…she had to be pretty drunk to enjoy sex at all. Anything she did, she did to please me."

It's so hard to say anything even slightly negative about a spouse who dies young. The person takes on a legendary status, enhanced because family members shared only positive or endearing family stories…and that was the way it should be.

But Anthony had told me these intimate things about Serena, seemingly without holding anything back. His story was the kind of conversation you have with someone you plan to spend a lot of time with. He'd allowed me to see the life-can-be-a-mean-bitch side of his life. You don't tell that to a passing acquaintance, especially if you're a control freak like Anthony.

"It was a little bit of an issue between us until…when she got sick, I pretty much put it out of my mind. It wasn't important anymore.

"And then you walked into my office. You had this…aura around you, like you were on a mission, and the air was crackling with your energy. It was like…you woke me up, like I'd been sleepwalking and going through the motions, and now I feel…" While we were talking, the tide had come in, and as he lowered his head to kiss me, a huge wave knocked us off our feet. I felt the wave pulling me as it receded, but Anthony held tight to my hand and dragged me, sputtering and soggy, to a spot where we were safe.

My stomach was churning with anxiety. *I have to tell him, I have to tell him, we have to talk about this! The man is pouring out his heart to me, and I have to be honest with him.* But I opened my mouth and nothing came out.

Suddenly he had a twinkle in his eye, and out of nowhere he started laughing, his whole body shaking. "You have a…" he was gasping for air, looking at my head. "You have a giant pile of seaweed on top of your head, it…" He was quivering and holding his stomach now, "…it looks like a crown or a wig or something!" I put my hand up to it and squeaked. It felt slimy and gross, and—eeewwwww—I couldn't bear to touch it!

Still laughing, Anthony plucked it off my head and threw it into the waves, pulling me up and walking behind me back to the hotel as he picked more of the leaves and pods out of my hair.

I felt my eyelids drooping as we rode up in the elevator, and Anthony picked up my hand and kissed it. "I think the adrenaline is gone and we need a little nap, don't you?" It was so sweet the way he insisted on slowly taking my clothes off, driving me a little crazy because he seemed to enjoy it so much. As he put me between the luxuriously soft bamboo sheets, I struggled to keep my eyes open until he slid naked behind me. *Mmmmmm, delicious.*

The sensual smell of vanilla chai and something cinnamon woke me, and Anthony hustled in with a tray of tea and cookies. "They were having high tea downstairs, so I brought us some." He stripped off his athletic clothes and got back into bed so we could feed each other cookies and drink tea in the buff. For some reason, his kindness felt overwhelming, and now it was my turn for a tear to slide down my cheek before I could hide it.

Catching the tear with the tip of his finger, he said, "Oh, my, look at you, Liz." He slid me over between his legs, my back to his chest, the sheet and his arms around me, his whole body around me as he leaned against the headboard. "I know why you're so sleepy and emotional Liz, and we need to talk about it."

I froze, one moment soft and relaxed in his embrace, the next stiff, tight, even trembling a little. "What do you...how, uh…" Taking a deep breath, I tried to turn and face him, but he held me, running his hands up and down my arms.

"I'm not going to let you go right now, Liz, because I know you're a flight risk. I don't want you leaving the room while we discuss the recent prescription for Clomid I found in your medicine cabinet."

Oh, shit, I thought. *I'm an idiot. He had a headache or something and went in there.* I closed my eyes, tilting my head back on his shoulder. "And you…I guess you…looked it up and saw what it was for?"

His hands were tight on my arms now, and I felt his jaw clench behind me. "I already knew what it was for, because Serena took it to have Leah. When I left your place in such a hurry, I was wondering…I needed to figure out…"

I pitched forward, pulling away from him, anger rising inside me. "You needed to figure out *what?!*" Wheeling around and facing him, the sheet pulled around me, I looked in his eyes and I saw it. Shame. "Oh, so you thought I was trying to, like, *trap* you, make you get me pregnant?! And then what? Did you think I was going force you to marry me or something?!"

He was silent for a long, painful moment, confirming my guess. "I needed some time. I mean, I get why you didn't tell me at first. It's not exactly first-date conversation that you're trying to get pregnant, but then as we got to know each other…

My mouth was literally hanging open. "How could you think…I would never do that to you. You know me, I'm a smart person, and I have my own money, I didn't need to trap you. That's just creepy and…and…crazy!"

"There's no doubt this whole thing is crazy. I mean, Viking sperm that comes in a cryovac package in the mail? And I didn't believe you would trap me. That's why I asked someone who knows you very well. If I didn't give a shit, would I have done that?"

"I guess you've been talking to Lilly, then. I'm going to kill her." But he had a good point. His conversation with Lilly couldn't have been comfortable.

Sinking down and sitting on the foot of the bed, I suddenly wanted to go over to him, wishing I could wind this morning back and replay, bring it up and discuss it before he had to call me out this way. "I kept *meaning* to tell you…" I knew I sounded like a coward. Which was accurate, because I had been a coward about this. "I thought about you so many times over the years, and in this precious time we were together…"

He held up a hand to interrupt me. "I knew something was bothering you, making you jump back into your safe zone all the time. When I was alone at my place, it was keeping me up at night. I was falling so fast, and yet I felt this *thing* from you, like you were always poised to leave."

Then I did crawl across the bed to him, snuggling next to him and covering us with the sheet. I *had* been wondering this morning when I would need to leave him. "I'm sorry. But I'm glad we'll talk about it now." That wasn't strictly true, because I'd been hoping for a carefree, sex-filled weekend but…as a distant runner-up? It was more than acceptable.

He reached over to brush my hair from my face and kissed the top of my head. "I know." He looked at the bedside clock. "Let's talk over dinner."

I wasn't sure a restaurant was the place to continue the discussion, but I nodded, and soon we were standing side by side in front of the beautiful stone vanity in the bathroom, wearing our white hotel robes. Grinning, I flicked some water at him and he flicked me back. "This is so couple-ish," I joked, glad he seemed open to it.

"I really like it," he replied, avoiding my eyes while he brushed his teeth. *Does he like it because it's me, or because he likes being part of a couple? He was married to Serena for so many years. How can I be sure I'm nothing more than Serena 2.0 to him? Gah!*

"I'll head down to the dining room while you finish getting ready. I want to get us a special table."

By special, I hoped he meant private, because it would be next to impossible to discuss Lars et al with the general public eavesdropping.

Chapter Seventeen

Liz

THE WAY MEN age is so unfair! Anthony was sitting at a magnificent table in a magnificent restaurant with a magnificent view…looking magnificent, of course, wearing his customary crisp white shirt, sleeves rolled up, and showing tanned, corded forearms.

The laugh lines at the corners of his eyes made him look interesting, not old. The silver hair at his temples only made him look hotter (and wealthier) than the attractive youngsters on the wait staff. Anthony's vibe was sexy, self-made professional, and every other patron in the fancy dining room screamed aging hippie who somehow made it big in software.

He quirked a smile at me as I sat down. "You know you look extremely hot, right?"

I was wearing a tight tribal print dress and the strappy heels I packed for a sexy weekend, not for a long discussion of my medical approach to procreation.

"This is my fifth-date dress. Did you realize this is our fifth date?" Each of our other dates had extended into multi-day sexathons, so the actual number might be somewhat unclear.

"Uh…okay. Is there significance to a fifth date?" He

leaned across the table and spoke in a conspiratorial growl. "Does that mean we can seal the deal and have sex now?"

The young waitress walked up right when he said sex, and her face was bright red while she quickly recited the specials.

"You look ridiculously hot, too, by the way, Anthony. I don't even want to discuss how many women are eye-fucking you right now. When did you get a tan?"

"Just through the windows of the helo and walking on the beach. It's an Italian thing. You look a little pink, me Irish lass. Jealous?"

I squinted at him, shaking my head. He seemed way too cheerful for a guy who'd suspected me of sperm robbery. "Irish and Danish, if you'll recall. My mother's people are from Denmark, and that's why I chose Lars the physicist as my sperm donor." I was giving him an opening to start asking questions.

"Lilly told me that, yes." He locked eyes with me and added, "Do you mind if we order our food before we get into that?" Anthony was a bit of a foodie and, always on his own schedule, he hated it when you didn't know what to order. The waitress rushed over when he looked her way. "We're going to share the seared foie gras, sashimi, Portobello sauté, and the veal chop, along with the 2008 Didier. Bring the food out whenever it's ready, no particular order."

"I remember when you used to order like that at a business dinner, and the food snobs from work would get all riled up."

"Are you saying I'm a food snob?"

"No, you're a foodie. A food snob would only order the foie gras and…mmm…maybe the peeky-toe crab 'cause they're expensive. You order everything you're interested in. You'd probably try duck vagina if it was on the menu."

"Is that a thing?" He made a face.

"In China it's a thing."

They brought the miraculous-tasting wine, and then each of the dishes, already portioned and arranged beautifully on two plates, one right after the other, the perfect interval apart.

A chocolate tartaletta arrived for dessert, and Anthony had them clear the table so we could position our chairs to take in the awe-inspiring view. There were only a few people left in the restaurant, positioned far behind us, so it felt like our own private balcony. At that moment a layer of clouds spread before us, covering the cliffs and ocean so completely I felt I could step off the terrace we were sitting on and walk on the clouds. "You didn't finish your wine," he said, a question in his voice.

"It was so delicious, I didn't want it to end," I sighed, putting the glass up to my face so I could enjoy its lemony bouquet. I knew I had a long dry spell ahead if I got preggers.

Laughing, he said, "Finish it. I'm ordering another bottle to go!" Maybe he wanted me a little buzzed for our talk, and I was glad to oblige.

We sat drinking our wine in comfortable silence for a while. The sky cleared, and stretched out over the ocean from our stunning vantage point, the leftover cotton-candy clouds luminous with colors of the setting sun. "So tell me the story," he said, stretching his long legs onto the railing. "Tell me when and how you decided to launch Operation Lars."

I gave him the whole spiel, starting with being the oldest of six, determined never to have kids. I reminded him of my relationships, and the role of career, family, and friends in filling the holes in my life. "Then two years ago, when I was staring at forty, it finally hit me. I looked into adoption, but decided I wanted the full monty, the pregnancy and birth of my own kid."

He pulled his chair closer to mine and took my hand. "And

why, in the midst of this revelation, did you decide to get in touch with me?"

I sat up straighter, the tears suddenly burning in my eyes, a sob tightening my chest. This nondisclosure to Anthony might have been the most gutless thing I had ever done in my life. I was ashamed of myself. Putting his hand to my mouth and kissing it, I let the tears come. "I honestly didn't confront that until this minute. After I set up this whole IU insemination, whenever I daydreamed about the ideal, perfect person I wanted to raise my child with, I thought of you."

At this point I was truly sobbing, filled with guilt while I stumbled around trying to apologize. "I remembered how you used to talk about your kids, and I realized it was exactly what I want for my child. The example you set, making a decision when you were so young, and seeing it through. I couldn't possibly admire you more than I already do. I'm so, so sorry. And I know I sound like an idiot.

"Then when you said things like 'I finally have money and time to spend on myself,' I realized my vision was just a fantasy." Holding his hand to my cheek, I confessed, "This morning, on the way here, I wondered how and when I could let you go so you wouldn't get hurt. Again, I'm sorry to put you in this position."

He took a breath to answer me but this time I kissed his cheek.

"I hope you'll accept it as a compliment, and not merely foolish manipulation on my part."

Chapter Eighteen

Anthony

THIS CONVERSATION—HER guilty feelings, and her confession about me—wrecked me.

Though I'd already decided what I wanted to say to her, her honest pain cut through me like a knife. I stood, grabbed her hand, and pulled her to my chest, kissing her forehead, then walking along the balcony with her. "Well, I'm sorry for saying those thoughtless things. I think I was unconsciously repeating what other people say, but not meaning a whole lot by it, once I gave it some serious thought.

There was a staircase descending to the beach, and I put her hand on the rail, the other around my waist. She was trembling, and walking unsteadily, her usual grace now reduced to pure grit. "Hold on, it's a long way down," I said, squeezing her and kissing her again.

I probably should have taken her back to our room, but I didn't want to be anywhere near a bed while we had this talk. Touching her was too distracting. This conversation was too important, and I wanted to be absolutely sure I said what I wanted to say clearly, so she would not only hear me, but believe me. I had to sell what I was about to say, convince her heart and her mind that it made sense.

What I had just realized today was that somehow, in our short time together, I'd fallen in love with Liz. The last time I fell in love was when I was sixteen. It was so long ago, I didn't recognize it. I'd *been* in love with Serena for twenty-five years, but this new version of falling crept up on me.

We sat on the bottom stair and took off our shoes, then held hands and walked along the beach while the sun was setting. I started the scripted part of my speech. "Though we've known each other for years, the biggest problem with what I'm about to say is that our current relationship is so new."

Liz looked at me, a hundred questions in her eyes. I had done jury trials, and this reminded me of the mind-blowing moment when the entire jury is focused on what you're about to say, and someone's future is on the line. This time it was mine.

"I've been having this conversation in my head since I found out what was going on with you from Lilly, so now I'm simply going to say it." I stopped walking and faced her, holding both her hands. "The truth is that I've thought about it, and I'd like to be with you, and be your baby's father."

"Be with me? And be..." She'd gone very still, and her mouth was opening and closing, nothing coming out, kind of like a fish. But prettier.

I rambled on so I wouldn't lose my nerve. "Well, I'd like to marry you, and I thought about doing the ring now, but decided instead to lay it out for you tonight so you can think about it. Only for a few days, though. I know you have an appointment with Lars next week, so you should decide before then.

"Lilly even told you *that*?!" I guessed she was so stunned by my proposal, she could only manage to cope with that tiny detail at the moment.

I nodded solemnly. "She'd never say so, but I got the distinct impression she's rooting for Team Anthony over Team Lars." Then it felt like I was railroading her, so I backpedaled. "Anyway…I know timing is important in this fertility thing, but maybe if you can't decide, you could at least skip a cycle and think about it."

Liz was speechless, her eyes were shining with tears, now shimmering in the moonlight. More words fell out of my mouth. "We are so new, and it feels crazy to say this, but I know you would make a great mom. Obviously, since I have a spotless track record, and I'm experienced, I can be considered an expert on the subject."

My relaxed smile in the face of her hysteria was making her smile too, though she tried to hide it. Pointing a finger at my face, she sputtered. "Just the idea that I…I still don't know how you could think so badly about me! Your sperm aren't that special!"

"I had to check it out. You know me, I trust, but verify. It's a Russian proverb. I actually think you like that about me, am I right?

"And by the way, my sperm *are* special. They're very fit, and excellent swimmers. With Lyndsey, they swarmed right past birth control. Serena had clogged pipes with Leah, but they overcame that too." Serena was such a huge part of my life it was important I learn to feel more comfortable talking about Serena with Liz. As important as her learning to be comfortable talking about Serena, too.

Liz was probably going to start asking pointed questions, so I decided it was time to distract her and go skinny-dipping. I took off my clothes and hung them on a rock. "Did you know it's much easier to talk about things when you're naked in the water?"

Heading for the sea, I looked behind me and saw her getting naked in the moonlight, a strip-off-her-clothes moment that would be burned into my brain for eternity. She ran toward me and splashed in, grabbing me from behind. "Is it really easier, or were you talking out of your ass Anthony?" This little inlet was warm and calm, and so salty it was easy for us to float.

I turned her toward me and put her legs around my waist. We kissed and made out furiously, exhilarated by the waves, the salty air, and the moon. "See? Don't you feel wild and alive? And yet there's no birth control, so you get to ask me a hard question."

Chapter Nineteen

I TOOK HIS invitation literally and asked the hardest question of all. "What would your girls think about us having a baby together?"

I know my eyes must have gone wide with shock when he answered "I've already talked to them about it. Lyndsey and I were at my place, but Leah was back at school in Philadelphia, so we included her via Facetime. She and Wendy had thoroughly talked out her initial reaction to you and the La Vida thing, and she even said she was sorry, which was huge for her. She's stubborn that way.

"She's figured out that no one I become involved with could or would try to be her mother, and she admitted she needs to get over it. She was quiet while I laid out the baby idea, typing away on her MacBook, so I guessed she was researching something profound about older parents." Anthony was trying to maintain a serious face, but there was a maniac twinkle in his eye about something. He kept rubbing my skin and swishing me around in the water to keep me warm.

"So Leah said, 'I mean, you guys are both old, so it's not

like Liz is our age or anything, that would suck. But the kid thing...weird, for sure. So is this going to be, like, a test-tube baby or whatever?'" Shaking with laughter as he continued, he was imitating Leah's attempt to sound indifferent. "Then she points to her screen like she's found the answer to World Peace. 'Hey, Mick Jagger just had a kid, and he's seventy-two! His oldest kid is forty-five, and he's also a great-grandfather!'"

"The three of us were laughing when I asked her, 'So does that mean it's okay? Because Mick Jagger is doing it?' She made a face, trying to deny it, but I think that's kind of what she meant. If we're not the only family in the world doing this, then it's okay with her. Somehow I'll have to convince her that, no matter what, she'll always be Daddy's little girl."

I loved the relationship Anthony had with his girls. I think my mom and I have it, too. It's very open. You can say anything, but you're willing to listen to the older person's experience.

"Still, you should think about it," I said. "Leah is about the age you were when you and Serena had Lyndsey. Wow." I was so proud of myself that I could finally speak Serena's name out loud in a conversation without feeling vulnerable.

And Anthony had said, "we're not the only family doing this," like it was a done deal. I have to admit, I loved the sound of that.

"Yeah, Leah actually said she was sorry for being a bitch to you before she got off the phone. She said she was happy for me. Lyndsey was another story," he continued, his arms tight around me. I loved the way he always touched me when we were talking about tough things. It was almost like he was afraid I was going to fly away. "Her question was more difficult. She waited until it was only the two of us. 'I want you to be happy,' she said. 'I like Liz, but I have some concerns,' is how she brought it up."

"Is she going to law school?" I asked, "'Cause she talks like a lawyer, don't you think? A very smart, grown-up lawyer."

"Hah, funny you should ask. She just took her LSAT, and she's starting law school part-time, because she wants her agency to pay for it."

I nodded. "She's smart, exactly like you. So what did she ask?" The ocean rolling around us was so pleasant, like a massage.

"She's worried a new baby would be the end of our original family. I asked her if what she really meant was, would Serena and the memories of our family of four be forgotten? That *is* what she meant, and the answer is no. I said we could handle it any way she wanted going forward, from counseling to maybe setting aside special times for the three of us to be together.

"I reminded Lyndsey about her best friend from grade school, a girl she's not in touch with right now except on Facebook. I said to her, 'It's not the same, of course, but the two of you were so close, and you still have those memories. In some ways, she's still part of your life, just like Mom will always be your mom.'"

It thrilled me how he seemed to have prepared so carefully for this conversation with the daughters…and this weekend with me. "It sounds like you presented this as something you and I are definitely doing. You didn't say anything to them like, 'If you hate the idea, I won't do it.'"

He drew me so tight to him you couldn't fit a piece of paper between us. "Hey, as you know, when you're trying to sell a new idea, you have to convince your investors you're committed." We both laughed, but there was more than a kernel of truth in there.

The air was cool when we got out of the water, and we rushed to put our clothes on so we could hurry back to the room and take them off again. Swinging my hand playfully in his, Anthony said, "I'm planning to use a condom tonight, so you don't need to stress about saying it. We'll continue this conversation tomorrow."

He seemed to have given this weekend so much thought, allowing me some breathing room to relax and enjoy it. I was grateful for that, no matter what the outcome. Maybe a word with 'come' wasn't the best choice after all this sperm talk, okay? So…no matter what I decided to do about Anthony's proposal.

The glow of the moon cast soft shadows on the balcony of our room. There were two frosty glasses of ice water with lemon and a bottle of champagne in a cooler near our private Jacuzzi. I was drawn to the exact spot where I'd watched the condor, knowing we were the only people in the world who could enjoy this particular view of the ocean, the moon, and now, the stars.

Anthony came close behind me, already bare-chested, and started pointing out constellations. "Look, you can see the Milky Way, and, oh, over there, Taurus! Wait, raise your arms, you can see Cassiopeia, up there to the right, so much better now!" He had been removing my clothes while he was giving his star tour, and now we were both naked.

His arms caged mine, four hands on the railing facing out to sea. Being here pulled together the infinite sky, the ocean, and our luxurious, finite little nest on this cliff. There was a faintly smoky smell mixing with the ocean breeze, a scent so peculiar to this part of northern California. "You seem to have so many reasons why things are easier when we're naked," I whispered. "I'm starting to wonder if it's only a sneaky way to get me to take my clothes off."

"Ya' think?!" he chuckled, kissing the back of my neck and then walking away for a minute. I felt so cold without him and arched my back when he returned, steadying myself on the railing and pushing my ass into his impressive erection. He hissed, losing his cool a little. He'd brought a chair and something else with him, but I didn't turn around, because not looking at each other felt right after our intense conversation.

"Not interested in astronomy, then? I could talk about chemistry if you want. We've got lots of that." He breathed into my ear, and his lips brushed ever so lightly over my cheek, his beard a feathery, erotic tool. I shivered when he ran one fingertip across my shoulders and down my spine. Goose bumps broke out all over my arms, and I gasped when his clever fingers touched ice cubes to my nipples. He palmed them under my breasts, and all the way down my ribs, the cold water trickling down my heated skin.

I pictured him smiling, enjoying my moans and torment. Putting the ice in one palm, he swiped the cubes between my legs, letting them fall to the floor when I flinched. "Let me warm you up," he growled, stroking his dick between my butt cheeks while his fingers moved in a circular motion over my wet pussy, massaging my clit and the wet lips of my damp slit, stroking every dip and curve. At first it felt so intense, his warm fingers and warmer cock where the ice just touched, his lips wandering over my neck and shoulders. "We ought to try having sex in a bed sometime," I groaned.

"Not 'having sex,' Liz, making love. We're making love. Be still, keep your hands on the railing like that, and let me play some more." He was sitting in the chair now, and I heard the rattle of ice before he traced a long, looping pattern on my bottom with the ice cube, the icy trail of water warming as it ran down my cheeks. I was whimpering and squirming, waving my butt and opening my legs to him. "Don't move," he snarled, and spread my legs even farther apart with his knees. I felt the delicious heat spread to my whole body from his hands, spread wide on my ass.

"I can't wait anymore, I have to feel you," he said, and thankfully I heard the tear of the foil packet from a condom.

"Oh please, yes, please fuck me," I groaned, shaking and already close to coming, my breathing quickening to a series of little gasps. His forceful thrusts lifted me right off the floor as he fucked me hard and fast from behind, touching fingers to my pussy, the other hand bracing my shoulder tight for the rough slam of our bodies. I loved the feeling of being full of him, of his muscles contracting against my back, and his beard whisking across my shoulder, raising goose bumps. When our bodies started to quiver and go stiff from an epic orgasm, he said "Keep your eyes open, see where we are!"

The effect, we agreed later while we were sitting in the hot tub, was like seeing your presents on Christmas morning, sensory overload with a warm burst of bright pleasure in your brain. "Except there's also a blinding flash of light and a jolt through your body," Anthony said, filling my champagne glass and proposing a toast. "Here's to your nipples. Without them your boobs would have no point."

His silliness made me spit champagne, and we caused a small tidal wave in the spa tub as we laughed and thrashed around for a good five minutes. "I love you when you're goofy like this, when you show how happy you can be instead of...hiding it," I gushed.

Pulling me onto his lap in the bubbling water, he asked "Is that the only time you love me?"

"Uh! I already said you were *always* more than special to me. I told you that on our first date! Now it's your turn!"

"Isn't it funny we haven't said it yet, the big L word?!"

Still holding me on his lap, I could feel his erection stirring below me in the water, but it didn't seem to bother him. *He was bringing up the L word! The terrifying L word!*

"Not that funny," I said. "Remember what I told you at dinner? This is only our fifth date!" With everything that happened today, it seemed incredible it was *this morning* when we climbed into that helicopter.

Anthony was stroking my hair, reaching behind me for the clip to pin it up. "I want to see your neck," he said. "I love your neck." Shifting me back onto the bench in the Jacuzzi, he turned toward me. "Okay, normally I would have written all this down, my summation to the jury about the times I've loved Liz Carleton before I realized it. As I said earlier, I only today figured out it's been so long since I fell in love that it sneaked right past me."

He squared his shoulders and took a deep breath. "I liked and admired Liz Carleton when she came to my office years ago, all smart and flirty, and when she created that program for returning veterans. I felt something change in me when Liz Carleton came to my office a few weeks ago, and I couldn't stop thinking about her. I saw how many people respect Liz Carleton…my people, and her people. I started loving her when I realized she created a home for some friendly folks who urgently needed a home, and when I saw how she provided a place where people can express themselves sexually.

"Okay, then there was the time in y*our* office, fucking against the wall, and in my Jeep, and my barn, and all those places. Can I call that love, or do I have to say lust? I love the way you walked around my vineyard with no clothes on, like you owned the place. God, my life was so boring these past few years!

"I even love your stupid pink drinks, and why you drink them, and of course I love the way you can't wait to touch me, wherever and whenever. You actually, truly love sex, and you're not shy about it. You're always looking for an opportunity to hook up, you're like a guy that way, but then in the process, you somehow…show me something about you…or about me." He kind of sputtered to a stop, but oh! Those lovely words!

"So do you get what I mean?" he asked, his expression hopeful.

"I absolutely get what you mean. I feel like I could spend the rest of my life living up to what you mean." We climbed out of the tub, and I handed him a towel, then thought better of it, starting with his back, and toweling him off all over, right down to his toes.

There was a fire burning in the fireplace across from our bed. I don't remember getting into bed, but when I woke up, the fire was a glowing pile of embers, and there was just a touch of light outside.

"Get up!" Anthony said, sitting bolt upright in bed. "We can watch the sun rise from the other side of the hotel!"

Chapter Twenty

Anthony

"LET'S DO IT, let's jump in the water." Liz said. She was wearing a teeny bikini that made me happy to stand around and stare at her, but she knew I was stalling. We'd enjoyed a lovely breakfast, walked the beach, and now we were watching people jump off two seemingly skyscraper-tall craggy rocks into the ocean.

"Jump off the cliff?" I was extreeeeemely skeptical.

"Yes, come on. You're a good swimmer, right? After you hit the water, you have to tread water until you catch a wave. C'mon, you can do it!"

"But…you used the word 'hit.' Hit the water. That sounds painful, especially when you have balls. What's the point?"

Hands on her hips, she pouted. "What are you afraid of?"

Even I had to laugh at myself. "Hey, I have dependents. Leah's still in school."

She was determined. "All the more reason to do it now, before you have another dependent."

I cocked an eyebrow at her because it seemed like she was saying yes to my proposal. We climbed up the steep rocks and stood at the top, wavering. The other divers urged us on, chanting "Do it, do it, do it!" Before we could talk ourselves out of it, I turned the tables on her, pulling her in close and kissing her, then gripped her hand and ran the three steps with her, right off the cliff and into the water.

Whooping when she got to the surface, she grinned at me. "Nut job!"

"Hey, it was your idea!"

We were treading water, waiting for just the right wave to carry us in to shore, when she looked down, confused. "Uh, Anthony?"

"Yes?"

"I lost the top of my bathing suit." The water was churning around us, no bikini top in sight.

I tried unsuccessfully not to laugh. "Ooops!"

"Huh," she said, lifting her chin above the water. "I didn't want any tan lines anyway." Catching a good wave without me, I watched as she strode out of the water, head held high, as if she went topless all the time. A couple of people stared, but hey...this was California.

Damned if she wasn't lying on the towel smiling, her rosy brown nipples on full display, when I got out of the water. Shading her eyes with her hand, she sat up and winked. "How do you like me now, *honey*?" We'd been calling each other silly names all morning, including sweetie, pookie, and, her favorite for me, stud muffin.

I dug her T-shirt out of our backpack and handed it to her. "Hey, *princess*, I don't want you to get a sunburn."

Making a face, she put the shirt on. "You just don't like to share, *Tarzan*."

"No, I really don't."

We walked back to the hotel hand-in-hand, energized from our leap of faith. "So...what happened to the Anthony who had more time and money to spend on himself?" she said.

"Did you talk with your sister about the crazy idea of becoming a parent all over again? Because before this, you didn't give it a thought, did you?"

I liked that Liz knew and approved that I confided in my sister. "Yes, the idea of you came first, the idea of a baby came second. Wendy says I don't know how to relax anyway, so I need a new project, and this would be a good one."

She laughed at that. "I like Wendy. A lot."

"Wendy got me thinking about what raising a kid would look like through your eyes. This wouldn't be like our parents, or like me and Serena when I was in the Air Force, raising kids, and balancing endless work so you're both treading water like maniacs. We're going to enjoy the world, and bring her along to enjoy it, too, but she won't be the only one having fun. Isn't that how you see it?"

Liz turned toward me and put her head on my chest, kind of bouncing her forehead off me. "That is so exactly how I see it, it's like you crawled into my head and put it into words."

"Does this mean you're accepting my proposal?"

"I think we should go back to our room right now and make a baby, I have a feeling about it," she said in a low voice I could just hear over the waves. "But..."

"But what?"

"Is it okay if we don't get married right away? I'm just...not ready for that."

I actually hated that idea. I've never thought of myself as someone's baby daddy, and I'm not going to start now. I decided to wait her out, resolved that at some point my persuasive powers would prevail, and she would marry me. I just knew the right opportunity would come.

Chapter Twenty-One

Liz

WE FELL INTO bed laughing, but it wasn't the edgy kind of passion we'd felt before. The room was warm and cozy, and we sipped wine and ate chocolate-covered strawberries off each other's bodies. Anthony teased me with light movements, slowly exploring my body with a hand here and his mouth there. I did the same. *This is making love, not chasing after an orgasm.*

Our eyes were open as we ran our fingers over each other, thoroughly kissing and teasing each other's mouths before we progressed to hours of tender, connected sex like nothing I'd ever experienced. He moved subtly, coming inside and circling, thrusting in shallow strokes and then deeper ones, my legs wrapped around him while we moaned and laughed and whispered about the things we were feeling.

It was so slow and conscious, yet at the same time intense and satisfying, as we tried different positions, above, behind, and facing each other, without having to worry about a condom. My brain was empty of all thought, just feeling with my mouth, my skin, and the places inside that clasped around his naked, beautiful cock. I lost track of how many times I came, and he did, too, staying inside me, motionless and calm, and then gradually becoming erect and going again.

In the middle of the night, we lay on lounges on our deck, covered with blankets and looking at the stars. We were quieter on the ride home in the helicopter, holding hands across the console when we could, and feeling comfortable enough to say nothing but mean…everything.

At home, we went to work every day but spent every night together, doing sexy things at the club, or nerdy date things. On the weekend, we went to museums, the Mob Museum, and the Las Vegas Neon Museum. We both love musicals, and we saw Jersey Boys, Rock of Ages, and all the Cirque de Soleil shows, condensing months or maybe years of dating into a few weeks. It wasn't "less banging and more dating," like we'd joked about before, it was more banging and more dating, enjoying each other in fast-forward, as if the mind games were over, because they suddenly were.

I called the doctor and told her to put Lars back in the deep freeze because the project was "on hold." When people asked what was up with us, we told them we were officially dating, and smirked about that label behind closed doors. In our minds, it was more like we officially had become one person.

Epilogue

Anthony

WHO KNEW A pregnant woman could be this horny? I was running out of ways to surprise Liz. She was always rubbing up against me like a cat, her breasts full and sensitive, and she was filling out and getting a nice baby bump, looking all lush and glowy, like the full moon.

Part of it might be she was allowing herself to nap every day, something the hard-driving executive of yesterday would never have done. Some women might think Liz had given up on being and having it all, and there might be some truth to that. As my fiancée said the other day, "You can have it all, just not all at the same time."

My sister and I both belong to professional associations, so we came up with the idea of forming an association of lifestyle clubs instead of expanding La Vida. Liz agreed wholeheartedly, since her motivation was to upgrade the image and profitability of these places so more people could enjoy them. She agreed to be the association's director for four years. Other club owners (from around the country and the world) loved visiting Vegas for the Adult Entertainment Convention and gathering afterward to compare notes.

I had a helluva time convincing Liz to marry me. I stood in the courtyard outside her apartment, playing *Marry Me* by Train on an old-school boom box, *Say Anything*-style. At first she came out on the balcony, made a sour face, and went back inside. She texted me *I'm still pissed you thought I wanted to steal your sperm and make you my baby daddy!*

Reading it didn't make a dent in my determination. Nor did it make me stop kneeling there, holding up her ring and playing the music full volume. Soon her neighbors started to whoop and holler, "Kar do!" "Dale un beso!" "Do it!" and a similar chorus of multinational phrases echoing through the courtyard.

When she came out again and cried, said yes, and came downstairs, I kept it gentle and dipped her over backward, just for effect, but when she came back up, Liz wasn't going to settle for gentle. Second time around, I didn't half-ass it, capturing that beautiful mouth of hers. She kissed me deeply, hungrily, and hooked a leg around my waist, as if we were going to get it on right there in the courtyard. The neighbors responded with more whistling and cheering, throwing flower petals from the bougainvillea and pebbles from around the fountain.

"I made you dinner, so I think we should finish this at my place," I said to her as we ran to my car, her eyes hot and full of yearning. She gave me pushy little kisses and touches all the way there, an indication of just how horny a pregnant woman she was already.

"Thank you for saying yes," I said. "I was going to be extremely uncomfortable going to the hospital with you as your...boyfriend? Lover? Sorry, but I hate that baby daddy shit! I know it's boring, but I want to be your husband, okay?"

"Anthony, my love, I realized that, and I got over myself." Her eyes were filled with tears. "You've surprised me, and

I've surprised myself. The loving things you've introduced me to, the affection. Endless. Surprising. I don't even remember the formal, uptight guy you used to be. I love you, stud muffin."

"I now pronounce you husband and wife. Anthony, you may kiss your bride!"

Father Murphy, our priest, was like an actor straight out of Central Casting, with white hair, blue eyes, and a face as big and ruddy as the side of a barn (with a map of Ireland on it). His arms were raised over us in a benediction that felt real, a blessing so heartfelt that every pair of hands surrounding us was compelled to clap enthusiastically.

When we met before the wedding, the priest laughingly assured me I was not the first obviously pregnant woman he'd joined in holy matrimony. Although at forty-one, I guessed I was probably the oldest knocked-up bride around.

English roses covered the beautiful arbor arched above us, Anthony's latest addition to our new vineyard. Of course, my mother cried from the moment the ceremony began. Was she remembering her own wedding, that moment so many years ago, before her six kids were born, when everything was possible, and love would never end?

After our kiss, I turned to see Mario hand my mother a handkerchief to mop up her happy tears. Funny, Anthony always carries a handkerchief, too. (Is it an Italian thing, or just old school?) My sisters were also handing out tissues, sitting with Anthony's daughters, his sister Wendy, and

Wendy's daughter Ally. There were seventeen pairs of crying eyes there in the cool of the desert evening, including my best friend Lilly.

Mario's son Primo and his wife Oksana, and my sisters' boyfriends Owen and Javier were having a good laugh at all the boo-hooing and mascara running down the ladies' faces. My father bounced my niece Abigail, our adorable little flower girl, on his knee. I was too happy today to dwell on the weirdness of my father and my mother's boyfriend coexisting in the same place.

And wonder of wonders, standing in the back of our little group were my twin brothers, Jack and Cole, shifting from right foot to left in that peculiar way we all use to soothe babies, rocking and bouncing my new nephews in their little blue caps and blankets. Jack's wife, Daniella, mother of the twins, sat next to them, her feet elevated on a chair while she enjoyed a moment of respite while hanging out with Tania, Cole's fiancée.

After Anthony and I greeted everyone, we led the party over to the food truck that regularly catered Oksana's show, a bright blue truck with a striped awning and a sign that read *Karina's Kufte and More*. Karina was ready for us with a big hug, and she waved us to sit down and enjoy her eastern European food, our wedding catering gift from Oksana and Primo. Served by Karina's cousins Nicki and Judy, otherwise known as the clowns Nicki Knockers and Big Booty Judy, the food was so fresh and delicious we heard people moaning audibly as they tucked in to the fabulous feast.

I pulled up a pair of chairs next to Daniella, one for my ever-expanding butt and one for my feet, and we decided this was the inaugural meeting of our Mothers' Club. She was a proud new member, of course, and my sister Sara was way ahead of us with my niece Abigail, six years old. "Do you think you'll try for a girl?" I asked Daniella, winking at my brother Jack.

"No," she answered, and Jack answered "Yes!" at the exact same time and laughed.

"Talk to me in about three years," Daniella said. She was so young she'd still be in her mid-twenties then, so it was realistic for her, certainly. Jack would be a little older than I am right now by then, but in that eternally unfair cosmic karma, it doesn't seem to matter how old the dads are.

Daniella and I were dressed in similar empire-waisted halter dresses, mine palest pink and hers black, the only profile that was flattering on a swollen belly. When she left to go into the house and breast feed the twins in the air conditioning ("Feeding them makes me sweat like a mother!" she chuckled), I sat back and took in the celebration, all the people I loved hanging out in the same place.

It occurred to me that every wedding, every minute of every wedding, is a cliché. It has to be. As little girls and young women, we've imagined this day, built it up in our minds...getting dressed in the unfamiliar yet intimately imagined white dress; exchanging meaningful glances with Mom, sisters, and girlfriends; and the look on your groom's face when he sees you in your new role as Queen of This Day. Even *I* managed to put on the false eyelashes and stuff my swollen feet into some heels.

No, my father did not walk me down the aisle. I mean, I'm back to *liking* the guy, but c'mon! The "giving me away" symbolism didn't work, since he was drunk or distant for least twenty-five of my forty-one years.

But my wedding day was imagined and reimagined so many times, it did feel like I'd been there before, sharing these tearful moments with Mom and my sisters and brothers.

Never thought I'd be carrying the next generation down

the aisle with me, but one of the good things about being an older mom is I'm too tired to lie about it. Think of the most tired you've ever been and multiply it by three…and the baby wasn't born yet. The other good thing was the absolutely definitive love you feel the second you see the bald, heart-beating image on the ultrasound screen. I felt my heart expanding daily to make room for Anthony Anzione the IV.

Yup. Anthony Anzione the IV is due in two months. Never thought I'd go for it, but we were doing the christening thing, using a gown passed down in his family, the whole bit. My mother was so happy she could hardly stand herself! I still wasn't sure what I believed about the whole religious thing, but it certainly was a comforting framework to operate in.

The person changed the most (besides me) by my fast-forward relationship with Anthony was definitely Lilly. I could see it. It had taken some of the sharp edge off her, given her hope there would be someone out there to share her future, too. Flopping in the chair next to me, she offered me a sip of her champagne, then gasped and yanked it away, sloshing, as if she'd offered me poison. "Oh, sorry, Mamadawg, no booze for you!"

"It's okay, of course not," I chuckled. "How's things at the Madame Lilly Poker Experience? The checks you're sending are very, very nice, by the way. Are you sure you're paying yourself enough?"

"Yes, ohmigod, I'd do it for free! I love living there, and I love doing what I'm doing!" Lilly quit her casino job, and she lives in Anthony's house in Red Rock now, making fancy breakfasts for the mostly male travelers who rent the place. Poker players—small corporate groups and older guys' bachelor parties—looking to get out of the casino atmosphere, find the property on Airbnb. Think classy bed and breakfast with poker flair.

She's styled herself as Madame Lilly, poker queen, playing like a shark when the unsuspecting vacationers need an extra player. Profiting tremendously from the rental fees and the poker, she was even toying with the idea of getting Lars out of the deep freeze and taking him for a swim, so to speak.

And the hefty checks sent for our percentage of the take helped to pay for the new vineyard Anthony and I started, where we grew different kinds of grapes than the ones in Red Rock.

Notice how I said "we" there. Who'da thought—Liz Carleton, er, Anzione, farmer? We bought this new property a few months earlier, thirty acres in the Pahrump Valley, south of Las Vegas. We only went to our offices three days a week, so Anthony had time to get the grapes started and fix up the new house. Our employees worked remotely on Mondays and Fridays as well, and everyone loved the new lifestyle.

I heard Anthony explaining the plan for the new vineyard to Javier as they walked toward us. "You wouldn't think wine grapes would grow here, but there's something special about the grapes grown in this dusty desert. There's an uppity word winemakers use—terroir. It means the environment the grapes grow in, and the way it affects the taste. We're only working on ten acres at this point, but the stakes are as high as any in Vegas."

They both happened to look up then, and had a good laugh at me, the pooped-out bride sprawled out on my chair with my shoes off.

"May I have this dance, babe?" Anthony asked, hauling me up out of my chair. We'd told everybody to start dancing without us, and they had, having a grand time getting to know one another, and taking turns dancing with Abigail and rocking the baby Carleton brothers, Jack Jr. and Daniel (I know, Jack Daniel, slightly tacky, but still fun). "Thanks for being my wife, wife," he murmured in my ear. The DJ played our song, Peabo Bryson and Regina Belles' version of *A Whole New World*, inspired by our epic helicopter ride.

Anthony had figured out a new way to dance with me, one arm around my shoulders, pulling me in tight, the other hand secretly spread out on my belly, catching the press of Big Sur's foot or his elbow.

Just like we had silly names for each other, Anthony and I had secret names for the baby. "The Fourth," obviously. Big Sur was a favorite ('cause he was going to be a big baby and that's where he was conceived), and Cliff, because having him was like jumping off that cliff—an act of tremendous, reckless faith in the future by two people who had every reason not to have any faith at all.

Excerpt from

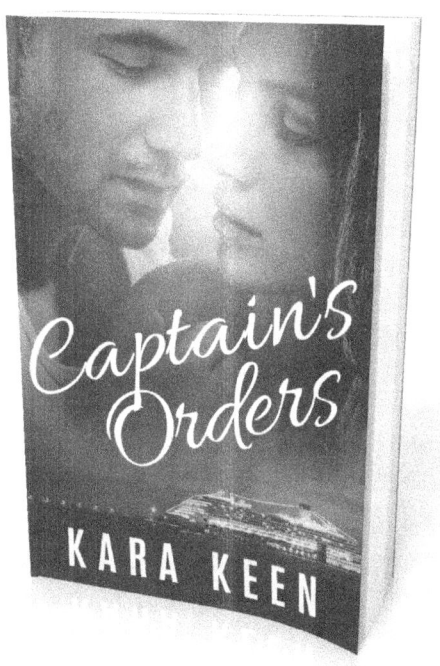

Let the sexy times roll!
Start at the beginning of the Captain's Orders series
with this excerpt from the story of Liz's twin brothers,
Jack and Cole Carleton.

Available in all formats wherever books are sold!

Captain's Orders

*She seduced the wrong captain,
and that's just the beginning…*

Cole Carleton, captain of the cruise ship *Sunset*, decides to capture Tania's heart after she mistakenly seduced his twin brother. After a night they'll never forget, he finds out what really brought her aboard in the first place. Is Tania only using him to rescue her sister, a young woman snared in a deadly web of international sex trade?

Tania Shevchenko will do anything to save her sister, and her sizzling attraction to the cruise ship's captain may be more of a distraction than an advantage. Proudly carrying her new American passport, she boards the ship and discovers there's more to life than working hard—and the sinfully sexy Captain Carleton is willing to be her guide to all of it.

Chapter One

COLE CARLTON LIKED to check out the passengers in the lounge while they waited to board his cruise ship, *Sunset*. It gave him an advantage over his brother Jack (essential between competitive siblings) and a chance to anticipate what problems and pleasures might be ahead on their voyage.

Wearing jeans and a T-shirt and carrying a duffel from his London shore leave, he fit right in with the passengers instead of looking like the captain of a ship with 3,000 passengers and 1,000 crew members. He was hoping to absorb the excitement while people checked in, their heady anticipation of an eleven-day luxury cruise around the UK.

Truth be told, he'd gotten a little blasé about the whole cruise business. It wasn't the intensity that bothered him, the challenge of keeping 4,000 people safe and 3,000 of them entertained. He loved that part of the job. It was…something else, a nagging feeling of being alone despite being constantly surrounded by people.

"And what part of cruising are you tired of?" Jack had asked him before shore leave. "Gourmet meals 24/7, seeing the world, the best gym on the high seas, women throwing themselves at us on every trip. If you asked most guys, they'd say we have the world by the balls!"

"Yeah," Cole frowned. "There's that last one. Don't you feel like shit sometimes? These ladies get off the ship and never think of us again."

"Au contraire!" said Jack, busting out his perpetual grin. "I think every time they're in bed by themselves, they think about us...a lot! And some of them come back for more!"

The young co-captains had a reputation on internet message boards for the attentive "customer service" they provided for single ladies on the high seas. They'd been profiled in the *Wall Street Journal*, the *Observer*, and *Le Monde* newspapers, but the full page in *USA Today* was the real kicker. A big photo showed the brothers smiling, captain's jackets unbuttoned, grinding a dance on either side of a lovely passenger who was wearing Jack's hat.

After they were interviewed by an attractive female host on *The Today Show*, she did an extensive feature covering her cruise hosted by—you guessed it—the Carleton brothers. The cruise line had been delighted—gave them a raise, in fact!

But Cole was tired of the lover-boy lifestyle. "You're okay with these women chewing you up like a fucking piece of man-cake on the buffet?"

"Okay with it? I love it! Bring on the frequent flyers, I say!" It was obvious Jack enjoyed flirting with every passenger in a skirt. It fit right in with his persona, the party guy who'll show a girl a good time—*this* week. Behind the mask, he was a shrewd judge of people and a quick study who'd schooled Cole through the maritime exams for their captains' licenses. When it came to women, though, Jack liked to leave emotion at the door. Numbness and indifference were easier than the effort and risk of an actual relationship.

When the main event was over, he was out the door, leaving the cuddling to Cole.

And control was not an issue for either brother once the bedroom door was closed. They shared…many things, including the ability to lead women down the edgy road to ecstasy.

But Cole had been feeling something else lately, a relentless loop running in his mind, especially after hooking up with someone. *It's always the same. You see someone, the eye contact thing, the flirting thing, hanging out, laughing, drinking. You hook up late at night and wake up alone the next day, feeling disconnected and lonely. Repeat. Drink, hook up, wake up alone. Repeat. What if there were something different? Something real I'm missing.*

He occasionally caught a glimpse of it in the eyes of older couples on the ship celebrating their 40th, 50th, sometimes 60th or 70th anniversaries. "What's your secret?" he'd ask them when he brought a bottle of champagne to their table. Some men would joke "Answer every question with 'Whatever you say, dear,'" but most couples talked about trust, honesty, support and the ability to laugh and have fun. They had a special glow and seemed to share an entire universe of growth, history and humor.

But right now, in this job, the single ladies kept coming, sailing after sailing. The twin thing was a big draw for women, always had been, even when they were teenagers. In their years as cruise ship captains, the brothers had teamed up with one woman, two—including a ridiculously high number of stunning twin sisters—and sometimes even more women. For a while it had felt like living the dream.

Recently though, after a few particularly wild nights, it'd started to feel more like a nightmare. Dressing in the bathroom of some woman's suite…again. Creeping back to his room and sleeping alone…again. *I'm the fling, the guy women sleep with before they meet "the one." My sisters think Jack and I are assholes. Are they right? If I find my "one," will I lie to her about my number? What is it anyway, have I slept with over 50 women? Fuck. If I tell the truth, will she feel I have no respect for women, no respect for myself?* Shoulders squared, arm stretched out as he pointed at his reflection in the mirror, Cole had vowed to end his casual hookups. *No more of that crazy shit. I'm done with it.*

He pulled his baseball cap down to avoid being recognized, dreading being back on board and dealing with problems extending way beyond getting the giant floating hotel from here to there. Could there be problems in such a fun, luxurious atmosphere? Yeah…

The tall, stacked redhead greeting the first-class passengers was one problem. Jeannette Taylor, the ship's entertainment director. Even though Cole and Jack had a no-fucking-shipmates policy, she'd made a play for them and ended up in the middle of the famous Carleton Brothers' Sandwich. Then for a while she'd expected to be on their regular menu. Big, big problem.

Cole watched as an older guy shouted in German, gesturing wildly at Jeannette. She expertly steered him over to the bar and calmed him, putting a glass of champagne in his hand. Leaning in so the obnoxious German could easily ogle her cleavage, she smiled and nodded while she listened to his complaints. *Nice work*, Cole thought when Jeannette led the German to the special elevator leading to the ship's largest suites. It wasn't officially time to board yet, but it was smart of her to hustle the high-maintenance rich guy out of the public eye and into his cushy suite. His unfortunate entourage, a tall guy with a shaved head and a pretty girl teetering along in ultra-high heels, followed close behind.

A white-haired gentleman a few yards away struggled to hoist his luggage onto a cart, and Cole considered whether to help him. He decided against it when the fellow's lady love handed him her bag and rewarded his efforts with a glowing smile. Grinning from under the bill of his cap, Cole looked forward to bringing a bottle of champagne to their table and asking their secret.

"Oooph," Cole had the wind knocked out of him when a big Middle Eastern guy stiff-armed him against the wall. *Problems, here come more problems.*

"Coming through," announced the well-dressed man behind him, barging through the other passengers as if they barely existed. Just as Cole was on the verge of protesting the rude behavior, he recognized them. The fashionable asshole was the Saudi prince the *Sunset*'s officers had been briefed about. Following close behind were his burly bodyguards and his burka-shrouded wives. They were bound for the Celestial Suite, the ship's largest and most luxurious. A tricky problem with this group was that other passengers felt uncomfortable when the women were herded around the ship like sad ghosts in their long black coverings.

Adding insult to injury, one of the sheikh's bodyguards threw the older couple's suitcases off the luggage cart, piled on the bags from the sheikh's wives, and pushed the cart toward the elevator. The sweet elderly couple looked dismayed for only a moment before Jeannette returned, bringing a porter and whisking them away from the ill-mannered offenders.

But who's this sweet thing? He watched as a tall girl with long dark hair and mile-long legs bounced back to her seat after registering. The woman had curves, something he didn't usually see in the leggy ones, and her teasing jiggle intrigued him. There was a quiet confidence in her long stride, strength in her posture, and she gave him a playful smile when he caught her eye. *Those eyes, long lashes pulling me into big brown eyes. And the lips, shit, full lips begging for a kiss.*

There was a prickly feeling at the back of his neck, an awareness that made it a struggle to look away from her. His anti-hookup vow flew right out of his mind and he grinned when she glanced back at him. Blushing a little, she looked down and then leaned back in her seat, staring intently at the private boarding lounge.

Still, her killer smile and a vision of her sweet ass, naked and ready for him to stroke and explore, distracted him from making his move. Long enough for a sophisticated-looking guy to sit down next to her, take her hand, and kiss it. *Dammit.*

Turn the page to enjoy another sample chapter as the fun continues! Cole and Jack return to their home for some time off in…

Excerpt from

Three sizzling affairs began on a cruise ship...
but what happens in Vegas might be more than the lovers
bargained for!

Available in all formats wherever books are sold!

Romancing Vegas

Oksana must transform herself from victim to confident choreographer and producer of the sexy Las Vegas show she's always dreamed of. Primo, who loves her, is with her all the way, risking his own life in a deadly grudge fight to finance the show. Will Oksana rediscover the passionate soul she learned to hide, or will the dark realities of her recent trauma drag her down, pulling the lives of her loved ones along with her?

Tania knew she was in love with Cole a few days after they met. They love hanging out, having fun, and working together to help Tania's sister Oksana develop a successful show. They also love exploring the electrifying edges of desire together. So what will it take for Cole to say those three little words, "I love you?"

Daniella didn't plan to fall for Jack, but she can't stop thinking about the crazy, sexy times they've shared. He's into fast, edgy living and so much fun—but is he ready to ditch the Peter Pan act and be her Number One?

What none of them know is that an old enemy lurks in the background, waiting for the right moment to take his revenge.

Chapter Three

OKSANA'S MOUTH FELL open and she grabbed Primo's arm, squealing with excitement when she saw the retro pink Cadillac convertible parked just outside the tavern. Aretha's *Pink Cadillac* played on the car stereo and the driver, dressed in a sparkly Elvis costume, held the car door open.

"Oh, my God, this is just...I cannot believe you remembered!" Sitting on top of the backseat as they drove away, Oksana waved goodbye to Tania and the gang like a beauty queen in a parade.

She'd shown Primo a magazine picture of a pink Caddy exactly like this one when they flew here from London. In the photo, a smiling, wind-blown couple drove the jazzy old car down the Vegas Strip, which was lit by the massive digital billboards of the hotels lining Las Vegas Boulevard. "That is my fantasy of Las Vegas," she'd said, and he laughed and started kidding her about it, busting her chops about the traffic, the noise, and the other tacky realities of the famous Strip.

But here he was, making her fantasy come true, his arm around her shoulders as they snuggled together on the cushy backseat. That was one of the great things about these big old cars—they had those broad bench seats, big enough for…well…anything.

Apparently Bruce Springsteen wrote *Pink Cadillac,* and the Boss's sexy croon was next on the playlist while the driver navigated back streets to avoid some of the constant traffic. They finally burst onto the Strip after circling Mandalay Bay, the colossal hotel at the far end.

She was wondering why he'd hired a driver until she felt Primo's long fingers wander from the bare skin of her shoulder, under the stretchy neckline of her top, brushing the tops of her breasts lightly with his fingertips. His confident, teasing touch made her heart pound with the naughtiness of it all. Their hips and thighs pressed tightly together, he reached across her and pushed the hem of her skirt up, finding the damp lace of her panties when he put his hand between her legs.

"Mmmmm," he purred in her ear, "How would you like to come while you see the sights?"

Oh, I would like it very, very much, but… "What about the driver?" she whispered. "He's looking at us in the mirror." She saw the driver adjust the mirror when Primo's fingers went down her shirt, his lustful eyes looking back at her.

"I don't think you mind. Your panties got wet like this when you saw him looking at you, when you realized that someone could drive up next to us and see us, didn't you?" He licked his lips, rolling her nipple between his fingers, his voice a low growl. "I'm getting to know you baby, to know what you like." He lifted the bottom of her shirt, ready to take it off, then paused. "And you like this. Don't you?"

Her cheeks burned at his question, but she trusted him and nodded, too excited to speak. He seemed to know instinctively where she wanted to go and how to take her there, an intuition shaped by hours of talking, touching, and building trust. The warm, humid breeze caressed her naked skin, stiffening her nipples when he removed her top and bra. Feeling so safe with Primo, and so totally alive, she actually relaxed, looking up at the constantly changing billboards, the leather seat against her back.

The music was Aretha again, *Freeway of Love*. Primo moved his hand to the back of her head, positioning her just so for a deep, toe-curling kiss that went on and on. His lips and tongue plundered hers, exploring every nook and cranny of her mouth, tasting like salt from the popcorn they shared at the arena.

This is it...this is what couples do. They spend time together and think of ways to surprise each other. This is right... Her heart did a hop, skip, and a jump as his lips closed around her tight, hard nipple, pulling it out a bit with his teeth, then flicking it. He made her ache with his tongue, nipping her and raining kisses up to her collarbone and the spot where her shoulder met her neck. Twisting with need, she opened the buttons on his shirt, rubbing her spikey nipples against his firm chest and pulling his head down for another urgent kiss.

She was hyperalert to their surroundings—yes, the dirty driver was watching, and no, she didn't care. The driver was playing Usher's *Bad Girl*, his commentary on what he saw in the mirror, she guessed. Looking over Primo's shoulder, she saw faces in another car. They were bathed in neon lights while they stared at the pink Cadillac, seeing only the back of the big man's head, a woman's hands on his shoulders. Her hands.

And now *his* hand brushed across the bundle of nerves between her legs. She spread her legs, whimpering for him to touch her pussy. She knew she was flooded with excitement, so she wasn't surprised when he groaned, "Damn, you are so wet."

When he pulled her panties aside, he fucked her with his fingers, sliding one finger, then another inside her. Curling his fingers in there, he found something sensitive and her clit responded when his thumb moved on it in small circles.

"Keep your eyes open and see where you are, sexy girl," he murmured, and she did, feeling slutty and completely liberated at the same time. While the lights and music of the Strip went by, he rocked her, touching that place inside and playing her skillfully, holding her as he clamped down on a nipple, sucking ruthlessly. Her belly pulled tight and her thighs shook as she whimpered and pumped her hips, begging for release. Waves of pleasure built as he pushed her, his touch demanding and consistent.

"Ohohohoh God," she moaned, turning her face into his chest to stifle her cry, but she came so hard her head fell back against the seat when a mighty orgasm tore through her. The night air cooled her body, her nipples still wet from his mouth. When her trembling quieted a little, Primo kissed her and pulled her top on, leaning in and stroking her hair.

"I...that was amazing," she marveled. "This is me wanting to do this, not some man telling me what to do. You make me feel safe, like *I* can do brave, crazy things."

"Well, good," he smiled, murmuring in her ear. "'Cause now I want you to do more brave, crazy things. Let's go in this club and dance and get sweaty. I know you like to dance."

Opening her mouth against his throat, sucking a little, she hoped she left a mark, hoped he would remember Oksana the brave girl when he looked in the mirror tomorrow morning. "Yes, I like to dance, I danced with you on the ship and in London. But I don't want to leave this club of yours without finding a dark place and fucking you." Her voice trembled a little when she said it; she'd never been this bossy before.

EDUCATING ANTHONY | 169

He was laughing into the kiss he placed on her forehead. "That sounds like fun. But does it *have* to be a dark place?"

"No, no it does not," she giggled. "And I like the way you think, beautiful man." He chuckled, as always, when she called him beautiful. He might not believe he was beautiful yet, but she was determined to convince him someday.

After driving the whole strip, they pulled into the brightly lit portico of Le Chic, one of the hip, small casinos she'd read about on the plane. The driver held the door open as they thanked him and got out, but when Primo handed him a big tip, he refused it. Careful not to look at Oksana, he said "No, thank YOU. It was my absolute pleasure!"

Breezing past an endless line of attractive people waiting to enter the club, they saw an official-looking guy carrying an iPad who waved at Primo. When someone in the line yelled, "Hey! Isn't that Gentleman Primo, the fighter?!" their host picked up the pace and rushed them into the hotel.

"I didn't know until tonight how…celebrity you are," Oksana breathed softly into Primo's ear. "Did I say that right?"

He laughed his rumbling laugh. "Uh, 'how famous' or 'what a celebrity' would be better. But yeah, there's this YouTube video, people keep watching it. That doesn't make me a celebrity, but whatever."

Before she had a chance to ask him more, they were in the elevator with iPad Guy, who asked Primo "Any idea where you'd like to hang out? I have your hostess ready upstairs, she's got your pineapple juice and vodka ready."

"Save us that spot on the balcony I texted you about, but first we're going to dance." The host checked his iPad, squinted at Primo, then nodded.

Thrilled that he'd made all these elaborate plans to make the evening perfect for her, Oksana leaned into Primo and squeezed his arm, knowing he'd understand. Then they entered the dance area and were hit by a wall of deafening sound—a mix of EDM, gangsta and current hit music—and a sea of writhing dancers.

Sweat gleamed on yards and yards of skin; since this was a beach club after 2 a.m., many women wore tiny bikinis and many men were shirtless while they danced like wild things. A three-story mirrored wall reflected hundreds of LED lights, but the towering mirror ball in the center of the room was what demanded attention. Rivaling a fireworks display, the enormous ball pulsed to the music, throwing off purple, green, pink and blinding white laser beams in intricate patterns.

It seemed to Oksana that the club was designed to help you escape, to forget not just your troubles but your actual identity. For tonight and tonight only, she was okay with that. Surrendering to the relentless beat of the music, she closed her eyes, threw her hands in the air, and lost herself in the club's sexy atmosphere. They were surrounded by long legs in high heels and glistening bodies vibrating to the intense music.

Primo spread his hands at her waist, rolling his hips and grinding into her from behind. Wild and shameless, she wiggled her ass into the zipper of his jeans. His hands slid under her skirt and he sucked in a breath, pulling her close and growling in her ear. "When did you take your panties off?"

"When you put our drinks down over there."

Nipping her ear, he murmured "So...in the middle of all these people?" She nodded.

He gripped an ass cheek under her skirt, one hand tight on her shoulder, holding her close as his big body pressed into hers. As they moved in a rough, seductive rhythm, his fingers slid forward to tease her pussy.

"And what did you do with your panties?" They both knew her skintight outfit was too revealing to hide anything. She pointed at a man dancing nearby who had her little red panties hanging out of his back pocket. Cracking up, Primo squeezed her buttocks. "You have been a very bad girl!"

"I know what you are thinking, but no, I threw them on the floor, kicked them away, then he saw them and picked them up." Turning toward Primo, she shrugged. "Maybe he thinks they will bring him good luck."

He picked her up and kissed her so fiercely she gasped. "I don't believe in luck, I believe in careful planning." Putting her down, he started pulling her through the crowd. "Now let's go to that dark place you talked about."

Primo had indeed planned ahead, tipping the club host so he and Oksana would be alone on the broad balcony overlooking the magnificent complex of rooftop swimming pools, an area on the eleventh floor known as The Beach Bar. Surrounded by tall palm trees and lit by an ever-changing colorful light show, The Beach Bar wouldn't open to clubgoers for about ten more minutes, and wait staff was hurriedly stocking the bars and bungalows, oblivious to the lone couple on the shadowy balcony.

Taking in the stunning view of the Strip and the Bellagio, Oksana leaned against the chest-high wall around the balcony. "How did you do this, Primo? How did you even think of bringing me to this beautiful place?"

Savoring the sexual tension that sizzled between them, Primo pressed against her again, his deep voice soft in her ear. "I've come here with clients, and it's not easy to provide security in this club. But I love being here with you." He turned her around and pulled her to him, studying her dimly lit face. "How are you doing with all this, you know…I mean, because you were a captive. Is any of this weird or scary?"

She stood straighter in his arms, shoulders back, a smile in her voice. "No Primo, no. I'm with you, I'm safe. This is so special and different for me. I feel hungry, starved for this night with you."

They constantly reassured each other like this, and she hoped someday her past would be a distant memory, not a frequent guest. Sliding the straps off her shoulders so her top slid down to her hips, she turned toward the wall that was vibrating with the beat of the music from the club.

When she looked over her shoulder at him she was blushing, but said in a breathy voice, "You know I've whispered about this, doing this with you, Primo. I'm so hot for you, please touch me."

Primo unhooked her bra for the second time that night and rolled it up, stuffing it in his pocket. When he lifted her skirt, her clothes were like a belt around her waist and he just stood there, enjoying the gloriously filthy view of her almost naked, where anybody could catch them. He stared at her, determined to touch every inch of her soft, smooth skin, and reached around to hold her perfect breasts in his hands while he pinched and rolled her nipples.

She trembled a little, and swung her hips in time to the music, nudging her backside into him. A fire burned inside him when he lowered a hand and worked her clit, feeling how wet and ready she was. Taking her right to the edge, he felt her legs begin to stiffen and she turned to him, panting. "Do it, Primo, fuck me right here. I do not care if they see, I want to show that you're *mine*."

"You're sure?" he asked harshly, raging lust driving him nuts. She'd often fantasized about doing this, whispering in his ear when they were both close to coming. He'd gotten caught up in it, and then *he'd* dreamed about it, the turn-on of knowing that someone might see them, could even be watching right now. "You want this?"

"Mmmm, so ready for you," she purred. When he yanked open his fly she reached back, her hand circling his cock, sliding it along her slit to wet it with her arousal. With a rough laugh, he played along with her teasing game, massaging that sweet button of hers with short little strokes.

The humid air was welcome, cloaking their skin with moisture for that extra slip, that feeling that moving together would be so easy. But it was never easy when a guy was as long and wide as Primo, and in this standing position, his chest to her back, the process was intense, just an inch, then a few inches. "Lean forward, baby, brace yourself on the wall."

Finally she let out a long breath, gasping at the broad heat penetrating her. Her beautiful pussy sucked him in, her abundant juices running down her legs, the walls of her sex tightening around him, his tireless hips rolling and thrusting like an archer searching for the bullseye. "Ooooh yeah, tell me when I find your special spot."

She stared over her shoulder at him, her dark brown eyes hungry and filled with longing. Panting, her lips loose, she murmured, "*Every* spot, every spot you touch feels special." It was a look he knew and loved, and he began to pound into her. Squeezing her ass cheeks in his hands, he watched the place where his cock entered her pussy. For a few minutes, the sight of that was the whole world to him.

Loud music pierced the air as the doors of the club opened downstairs and the revelers poured out, a few pulling off their clothes and jumping in the pool while most accepted free glasses of champagne from pool staffers in pirate outfits.

There was noise, but not enough to cover Oksana's cries, which rose above the music as she quivered when his fingers found her clit, his body sheltering hers while he continued to drive into her, whispering dirty words of pleasure in her ear.

The emotion of it crept up on him, the intensity of this mission to explore their fantasies, her resilience after the bad things that'd happened to her. When she turned her head and he looked in her eyes, they held the perfect combination of sweet and lewd. He felt his heart race and his cock pulse, the beginnings of his orgasm. An unfamiliar desperation crept up on him. *No, no, I don't want this to end.*

He slowed the pounding, focusing on her again as she bucked her pussy into his stroking fingers. Her hips moved from side to side, and when he tightened one hand at her waist, the other at her neck so he could grind tightly into her, her pussy contracted strongly around him. She gasped, "Primo, ooohh, I'm coming!" A cluster of people below looked up toward them, each person elbowing the next and pointing up at the balcony.

Boom, pop, pop, bang, ba-BOOM! Colorful fireworks began to erupt at the other end of the pool, distracting the nosy watchers and everyone else on the pool deck. He and Oksana felt the deep boom vibrating the balcony they were standing on, and the sound was deafening, pulling Primo back from the edge a little. But they were free now, free to explode and release the pressure inside as loudly as they wished.

Still, it was impossible to ignore the turn-on potential of their audience, real or imagined, and Oksana stood straighter, her face and breasts and Primo's shoulders reflecting the brilliant colors of the fireworks and the lights. He continued his blissful torture of her clit and breasts, enjoying her desperate little sounds and making her feel every inch of his cock as he thrust in quickly and pulled out slowly.

"Someone is watching us right now," he breathed into her neck. "They're above us or behind us and they're touching themselves because they can see us. They can see your breasts and your beautiful legs and they know you're going to come again, they can see it in your face."

That was all it took for both of them. She let out a cry of ecstasy, her body shaking from the intensity of her orgasm. Seeing, hearing, and feeling her, he roared and erupted inside her, the sound swallowed by the thunder of the fireworks while waves of orgasm rolled through him. Leaning heavily against each other, they gradually untangled and stopped shaking, but were still reluctant to part, to pull their warmth away from each other.

Their clothing still messy, he shielded her while they looked around them, tugging on their clothes and smiling.

"Isn't it funny how suddenly...how you are aware of things when it is all over?" Oksana giggled.

They managed to get sort of pulled together just as people started coming out onto the balcony toward them. Several couples joined them at the rail to watch the fireworks. One woman winked at Oksana and gave her a thumbs-up. *Hmmmm.*

Continue the adventures of Oksana and Primo in
Romancing Vegas!

Kara Keen

TOP 10 AMAZON AUTHOR

After a career in public relations and advertising, Kara Keen got tired of writing half-truths and decided to write the whole truth—love is all you need!

Placing her characters in exciting destinations, she enjoys guiding them through emotional situations and sophisticated adventures. More importantly, readers and reviewers of *Captain's Orders* and *Romancing Vegas*, her first two novels, appreciated how her characters heal each other through wise-cracking humor, honest talk, doing the right thing, and really hot sex!

Kara wrote two nonfiction books (under a different name) about sex, intimacy, and women's health, and spoke at conferences across the country. Recognizing that the brain is a woman's most important sex organ, she started writing stories to fire up women's minds about the many ways men and women get together. Hanging out with her family in northern

Virginia, she has no problem sharing the secrets of writing—read a lot, connect with other writers and keep your butt in the chair until you reach your goal for the day! As writers and most professions will agree, it's not just a matter of inspiration but of perspiration (putting in the time and effort).

If you enjoyed *Educating Anthony* and want to go back where it all began, read *Captain's Orders* and *Romancing Vegas*! Yes, *Romancing Vegas* does feature a cameo by Liz, but you'll have so many new characters to love—Primo and Oksana, Tania and Cole, Daniella and Jack. They are totally different and unique stories you'll love. Can the sex get any hotter? You'll have to find out for yourself!

CONNECT WITH KARA ONLINE:

My Website—http://www.Karakeen.com
Facebook—http://facebook.com/karakeenauthor
Twitter—http://twitter.com/karakeenauthor

If you enjoyed reading *Educating Anthony*—please recommend it and review it. If you do review the book on Goodreads or your favorite retailer, feel free to email me and let me know.
KaraKeen.author@gmail.com

www.ingramcontent.com/pod-product-compliance
Lightning Source LLC
Chambersburg PA
CBHW071243130626
46556CB00003B/1146